A WINSTON & CHURCHILL CASE

THE SHADOW OF VICTORY

THACHER E. CLEVELAND

FIRST PRINT EDITION

ISBN: 979-8-9910961-1-9

Foreward

Before we get started, let's take care of the elephant in the room.

Yes, this is the fourth volume in The Winston & Churchill Case Files. The previous three volumes are their own trilogy, and while the effects of it are felt in this installment you don't have to have read those before reading this one (provided that I did my job right). As someone who has spent a lifetime reading comic books, I'm acutely aware of the need for entry or jumping on points for an ongoing series. While this series doesn't have the fifty plus years of stories a Batman, Spider-Man, and their associated friends (amazing or otherwise) have, I felt like it was a good idea to make this one of those points. If you read this and enjoy Henry & Martin (and/or are curious as to where Lexie is), you're more than encouraged to go back and read the previous collections.

Yes, this is also a sequel to my first novel, "Shadow of the Past." I suppose you don't have to have read that to enjoy this, but be warned there are spoilers aplenty for it in here. So consider yourself warned. I've tried to provide the basics of what happened in a non "info-dump" kind of way so you don't feel lost (or if it's been a while since you read it).

Okay, thanks Mr. Elephant. Moving along.

It took me roughly twenty years to write Shadow of the Past. To be fair, I wasn't writing it the whole time, and I even had to completely start over around the ten year mark as the floppy disk I had it saved on crapped out, but it was a long journey. Once it was done I shifted gears pretty quickly to other assorted projects, and while it was the first physical book I produced I leaned pretty heavily into the Winston & Churchill series.

In my mind, Shadow of the Past and the Winston & Churchill stories always took place in the same "universe." I've always loved that kind of stuff even before it became as ubiquitous as it is now (see the above remarks about reading comic books my whole life). Martin was always from Cedar Ridge, and I knew that age-wise he'd be relatively close to Mark and Christine, so consciously or not I laid the groundwork for the "crossover" from the get go. Knowing that I am the way I am, it really was only a matter of time before it happened. With Covid providing a good stopping point for the Winston & Churchill gang's adventures for a bit, this seemed like as good a time as any for it to happen.

I had heard from some folks who read Shadow of the Past that they hated the ending. Not because it was bad, they assured me, but because it left Mark in a pretty dark place and not-so-great circumstances. Given everything that happened in that book, it felt like the only way things could have been resolved. Hopefully those people will be satisfied at what's become of Mark (and Christine), since then.

Although, let's face it, having your friends and loved ones murdered when you're a teenager is going to have some lasting effects, so don't be surprised if it's not all sunshine and roses.

So with that said, on with the show...

Chapter One

"Fuck Covid!"

It was at least the fifth time it'd been yelled, but it still drew a large cheer from everyone at the party, temporarily drowning out the heavy bass of the track shaking the foundation of Tim Meyer's house. Martin Green hadn't been close with Tim in high school, but after almost a year of being trapped in his parent's house he was ecstatic to see anyone but them. It turned out "anyone" included the privileged choad he'd had four years of homeroom with, and who was also the kid who crashed the SUV he'd been given for his sixteenth birthday six weeks after he got it. And then the replacement he'd gotten two months later. Then it was just a regular old Mercedes. New, not used, of course.

Martin's need for a parent-free zone overruled his annoyance at Tim being handed a whole-ass house this time. Once the pandemic got into full swing his parents permanently moved to their summer place in Martha's Vineyard and Tim had himself a whole new place. Martin had almost left when he found out Tim worked in some sector of finance and managed to make money in the last year and a half. Meanwhile, Martin had walked the two and a half miles there so he didn't have to pay for an Uber twice in one night.

Human contact was human contact, though. He'd been a little surprised the invite had found its way to him, since he'd been staggeringly unremarkable in high school. He'd been a quiet, anxious, and gangly teen with a pretty small social circle, whose only extra-curriculars were editing the art and literature magazine and being vice-president of the Jewish student union. He hadn't even been invited to many parties back then, but now he was less-quiet, still anxious (but medicated), and had grown into his slender frame he was ready to give this a shot. The warm feelings of inclusion had cooled significantly when he realized practically everyone in their class had been invited, and with reunion the upcoming weekend (after being delayed because of Covid) there were plenty of others from the adjoining classes of Cedar Ridge High as well.

He might have turned back into a shrinking wallflower, but at least there was enough free alcohol to take the edge off.

"Marty!" Tim yelled, emerging from the crowd and throwing an arm around Martin's shoulder. "How the fuck are you, bro?"

"Good, good," Martin said, leaning away from him not out of fear of infection (he'd been double-vaxxed as soon as possible) but to escape the cloud of liquor breath and second-hand weed-smoke he exuded. New Jersey's recent marijuana legalization was also being celebrated, and in an incredibly vigorous fashion.

"But what have you been *doing*? Like, I know it's not our reunion, but we should, like, reconnect and shit. Give me the deets, brother."

Martin downed the rest of the drink in his solo cup, trying to figure out how many deets he should actually share. "Not much. Just an office job."

"Yeah, but in the city, right? Jen Robards said you were working for a cop or something?"

"A detective agency," he corrected. The Robard's friendship with his parents had always been a thorn in his side, especially since Jen was now a resident at Mt. Sinai. "I'm a...," he almost said 'secretary,' the word thrown at him by his parents in their most disappointed tones at least once a day. "I'm an *associate*."

"No shit!" Tim cried, throwing his arms into the air and giving a chance for Martin to duck out from under his grasp. "I'm an associate too, dog!" Martin faked a smile and gave Tim the high-five he was craving.

"That's fuckin' dope, dude. Associate bros! Finance and...wait, you said detective? Like Scooby-Doo or some shit?"

"Remarkably similar," he said, realizing Tim was past the point of being able to retain any long-term information. "Lots of monsters, definitely some ghosts. Not enough old white guys in masks, though."

"Fuckin' wild, bro. Like...how do you get into that shit?"

"I had a bad break-up and used magic," Martin shrugged. "Turned myself into a demon-gorilla thing. Now I'm studying how to do it for a living."

Tim had been staring off into the crowd, nodding along, and then some of what Martin had said must have sunk in. "Wait...what? With like...scarves and bunnies?"

"I wish," Martin said, patting him on the shoulder. "Anyway, I gotta go see a guy about my sanity." He headed for the makeshift bar, leaving Tim to bro-out with another of his guests. The ridiculousness of the truth, coupled with the trauma of memory, had left him thirsty. He took another solo cup of what had been labeled "Drank," and parked himself in a corner, memory and alcohol gelling into melancholy as he realized this was absolutely not the human contact he'd been missing. Tim may be the money-making kind of associate and live in a spacious, modern, and basically free home, but at least Martin was able to consider his bosses friends, and felt like they actually respected him.

Well, definitely Henry. Probably Lexie. Maybe.

Both had reached out to Martin on his birthday a few weeks ago, and even though Lexie's move back to upstate New York was supposed to be temporary, it'd been just over a year now. Henry had been working on some small cases on his own for his wife's law firm, but things had slowed down considerably. The other side of the business, the "Scooby-Doo shit", had ground to a halt as well. With things returning to normal he knew it wasn't going to stay that way forever, and handling their unique brand of danger without Lexie's help made him queasy.

He'd tried to push Henry to teach him more casting during their time off so he could do more than just research, answer phones, and digitize a twenty year old file system, but there wasn't much more he could learn over a Zoom call. His own ability to study and practice was hampered by his parent's constant and overwhelming presence, not to mention how freaked out they'd be if they saw him with any supernatural paraphernalia.

Martin had taken a spot at the end of the hallway toward the back of the house, right across from the wide archway leading into the massive living room space dominating the first floor and where the bulk of the party raged. It wasn't what he'd had in mind for his night, but at least the people watching there was good even if the music from the over-powered sound system wasn't. He was about to get another refill when a heavy burning smell hit him full force. There was enough space around him he didn't think it was coming from anyone in particular, but as he looked around he could tell it was coming from behind the closed door he'd been leaning next to.

He opened the door a crack and the smell lashed out at him so hard he stumbled backward and bumped into a guy passing behind him, spilling his drink

"Whoa, man!" the guy said, and then recoiled as he experienced the scent as well. "Dude, rank!" He scurried away, glaring at Martin over his shoulder.

"Sorry," Martin said, flushing in embarrassment. "It wasn't me though!"

Martin opened the door wider, risking further blame. On the other side was a set of stairs going down about half a flight and then turning to the left. Whatever might possibly be on fire was down around that corner for sure. With no Tim or someone Timadjascent in sight, he placed his cup on a table and headed downstairs.

"Hey, is everything cool down here?" he said when he reached the landing, trying to make sure he was neither screaming or whispering and somehow failing at both. The light he'd found on the stairs was dim and didn't reach the room below.

There was no response.

"Yer a wizard, Marty," he said to psyche himself up. Lexie had started teasing him by saying it in the months before she left, complete with horrible accent, and remembering it encouraged him to walk the rest of the way down the stairs.

When he turned the lights on, it was clear the well-furnished basement was empty. The space was large and ran under the whole house, and was decorated like a frat house inspired by Scarface. An uncomfortable amount of naked and nearly-naked pictures of women covered the walls. Where there wasn't nudity there was neon signs of various beer brands and slogans that, among other things, reminded him to "Be the Alpha." There was a pool table and bar to his right and a home theater system on the far wall rivaling the one upstairs. If it wasn't for the overwhelming stench of old barbecue and trash he'd have wondered why the party hadn't spread down here. Across the room was the only other door, which stood partially open, and the room beyond it was dark.

He walked towards it and then stopped halfway. The smell was stronger, and most certainly coming from there, but there was no glow of flame or heat coming from it. Martin tried to let his eyes adjust so he could see what was beyond the doorway, but nothing revealed itself. He took another step and a rush of cold spread out from the center of his body, stopping him. He tried to convince himself it was from the alcohol and hits he'd taken making him paranoid, but the familiarity of it made him think it was something else. He waited for it to go away, and when it didn't, he turned around and headed toward the stairs. The feeling faded as fast as it'd come on, and he convinced himself it was nothing to worry about.

Behind him, the door closed.

"Oh, come on," he said. The feeling returned, more insistent than before and strong enough to sober him up some. He looked over his shoulder, and while the door had closed there was still a thin crack to remind him of the darkness beyond.

"This is fine. This is *fine*," he said to himself, walking carefully back toward the door.

"I'm sure you're just some folks having a good time," he said loudly as he approached. "But please don't be fucking or about to do a jump scare. I don't consent to either thing."

There was no reply, and the smell had either begun to fade or he was somehow getting used to it. He pushed the door open with the barest touch of his fingertips, body tensed to run at the slightest surprise. When there was none, he reached around and felt for a light switch. Turning it on revealed the room beyond was barely five feet square, with a stacked washer and dryer, small wash sink and cabinets on one side, and a laundry chute on the other.

"Alright then," he said, taking a few steps inside and then nodding to the laundry chute. "That's tight, though. You don't see a good chute nowadays." The smell got stronger but it didn't have the physical force behind it like it had before. If anything, Tim had probably tossed filet mignon not to his liking down into the laundry room. Looking at the overflowing piles it was clear they'd been left alone for a while. "Motherfuckers haven't even *earned* a chute," he grumbled.

There was a heavy thud above him and the overhead light went out.

"Shit!" he jumped back, clawing for where the switch was. He flicked it a few times but the light didn't turn on. The room shuddered with another impact, this one coming from all around him, and then something lit up behind him.

He turned and saw the inside of the dryer in flames.

"Oh, come on!" he cried, the heat overwhelming him and making him stumble backward. The dryer door was closed and the window was browning and warping, the plastic edges already starting to melt.

He opened his mouth to yell but the flames sputtered out, leaving behind a massive cloud of smoke and the the lung-burning return of the burned meat odor. His eyes were burning and he waved away the smoke, trying to assess the damage. Despite everything, there was a panic at his core at how this was his fault for messing with the lights. Most likely, Tim would want him to replace them with the fanciest and most expensive ones in existence. The inside of the dryer was still thick with smoke, and he reached out tentatively for the deformed handle in case it was still hot.

A hand slammed against the window from the inside.

"Dude, what the fuck!"

Martin shrieked, tripped, and fell on his ass. The hand pushed door open, letting out waves of smoke and stench. The hand, and the arm it was attached to, flopped down against the front of the washer with a wet slap. The entire thing was horribly burned, the skin blackened and cracked all over, and in some places scorched down to the bone. The smell was charred flesh, he realized, and it was now so fresh and powerful a primitive part of his brain remembered he hadn't eaten earlier.

The burned hand twitched, the exposed bone of fingertips clicking on plastic until they found purchase and began to pull itself out. A head, shoulders, and second arm emerged from a space they shouldn't have been able to fit in to, and all of it was just as burned. The head, which looked like a peeling lump of over-cooked shawarma meat, lifted up and there was a hole where his right eye should be, tunneling all the way through the skull to an even larger hole in the back.

There was a shift of meat and the bloodshot, but otherwise undamaged, remaining eye appeared. More sliding meat sounds and teeth, cooked like steak bones, were exposed in the worst and meanest smile imaginable.

"Great party, huh Marty?" it gurgled, the voice rough and male.

The thing pulled itself forward more, exposed ribs rattling like a xylophone against the bottom of the dryer's opening until it flopped down at the waist, palms resting on the ground. With most of it out of the way, Martin could see the inside of the dryer stretched back impossibly far, with dancing flames in the distance like a warp-pipe to hell.

"Do you see it, Marty?" the thing said. "Can you see Him?"

Even with its ruined, impossible voice, Martin could hear the reverence in "Him." Martin crawled backwards as the human turducken pulled himself fully out of the dryer and started to crawl forward.

"He can see you," it continued. "He can see you and you're just what he needs."

The burned hand reached for Martin's shoe, only a couple inches away but close enough to bring him to his senses. His attempt to spring up to his feet ended up as a half-crabwalk, half-cartwheel, and he had to flail his arms wildly to stay upright. Despite being a burned corpse, the thing got to its feet with less of a struggle.

"He's going to love you, dude." It made a noise that could have been a laugh. "I bet you're fucking delicious."

The extreme terror did a great job of clearing his head of drugs and drank, and he took a deep breath and held out his hand, palm facing out.

Yer a wizard, Marty, he remembered.

He closed his eyes, focused his intention, and under his breath he recited the words to the most powerful ward he could channel. He felt a push against his outstretched arm and he planted his back foot, leaning into it.

"I *am* delicious, motherfucker."

There was another push and then the resistance was gone, fast enough to almost make him fall forward. He opened his eyes and the thing was gone, the only smells now an overabundance of Febreeze and dirty laundry. Across from him, the dryer was flame free and undamaged. Martin's body ached and his appetite had returned and brought friends. He backed out of the laundry room and towards the steps, not taking his eyes off the dryer. When he felt his foot hit the bottom stair he reached for the switch while he flipped off the whole room.

"Yeah, you better run," he called, turning off the light with a flourish and hurrying up the stairs. He found Tim and his brother right away, holding court for a group of guys that were definitely still in high school and completely enraptured by them. "Hey," he said, putting a hand on Tim's shoulder and interrupting. "Can I talk with you two a second?"

"Kind of in the middle of something here, bro," Tim's brother Eric groaned.

"You'll survive," Martin said, not looking at him. "Tim, it's kind of important. There's something going on in the basement."

"Oh shit," Eric laughed. "Did you see a ghost?"

That got Martin to look at him. "What are you talking about? What ghost?"

Tim shrugged Martin's hand off his shoulder and rolled his eyes. "It's bullshit. A couple of our housekeepers said they heard something down there, or smelled something, or whatever, but we never find anything."

"Just excuses," Eric said, looking over at his assembled pupils. "We had to get rid of two of them in a row. No one wants to work any more. They got handouts over the pandemic and now that they got a taste they want to live off our tax dollars." The student body nodded in solemn understanding.

"Do not listen to this corporate trash," Martin said, pointing at Eric and turning back to Tim. "Did they say anything else? Anything specific?"

"The fuck should I know?" Tim said. "You think I chat with the help? It's gotten so weird and funky I don't even go down there anymore."

"Try to remember," Martin said, beginning to lose his composure. "It's important."

"They wouldn't be able to see it," one of the teenagers at the back of the group said in a familiar voice. He was tall, white, and sandy haired, standing so Martin could only see his left side. "And you were right. You're *scrumptious*."

He turned his head, and Martin recognized the fist-sized hole through the right side of his head.

"Fuck," Martin whispered.

"Fuck what, bro," Eric said, turning to look right through where the as-of-yet unburned teen stood.

"He's going to have so much fun with you." The teen smiled in a way somehow worse than before. Martin started backing away and the teen saluted him with his solo cup, then took a drink. As he did, the skin around his head-tunnel caught fire. It spread quickly, up to his hair and down onto his clothes.

Martin raised both arms and drew in what energy he had left, but it was immediately apparent what was left didn't amount to much of anything. The now fully immolated teen walked toward Martin, and the heat was withering and the smoke so cloying he almost fell over.

No one else could see or feel it, making Martin's stumbling retreat look insane. A tide of "Dude"s and "What the fuck"s rose up as he pushed toward the front door. The crowd was the only thing keeping him from sprinting, and he risked turning away from the thing so he could go faster.

"Sorry," Martin said, shoving through them and feeling the hair on the back of his neck beginning to singe. "I need some air."

When he got to the front door Martin looked back. The flaming teen had effortlessly moved through the crowd without anyone noticing him, although a few people he passed looked around for where the faint burning smell was coming from. Martin yanked the door open and stumbled onto the lawn, gasping for clean air, and he didn't turn around until he was on the sidewalk.

When he did, he saw the thing standing in the doorway, waving at him. "See you soon, Marty!" it called out. "He'll see you real soon!"

Martin pulled out his phone and went to his contacts. The line rang for a few moments, and then Henry picked up, despite it being just after midnight.

"I really hope this is important," he said, obviously having just been woken. Martin looked back up at the house and there was no sign of the burning teenager, although he could still smell the smoke all around him.

"Yeah," Martin said, taking a breath. "You could say that."

Chapter Two

Henry Churchill checked himself in the mirror one more time. He was still Black, short, and more overweight than he'd like but, unlike the most of the past year, wearing one of his suits and dress shirts. He adjusted the glasses he was still getting used to wearing, the unfortunate by-product of closing in on his forty-eighth birthday. Being properly dressed and not in his regular "stuck at home" uniform of sweatpants and a t-shirt, did wonders for his disposition.

"I've got to head into Jersey today," Henry announced, emerging from the bedroom.

His wife Monica, sitting in the breakfast nook of their apartment on Manhattan's Upper East Side, looked up from her tablet, eyebrow raised.

"I take it this has something to do with the call you got last night?"

"Sorry," he said, giving her a kiss on her forehead. "I didn't think I woke you."

"I know," she said, turning back to her reading. "I'm just glad you didn't take off right away. Martin?"

"Yeah," he said. "He was pretty freaked out."

"I should hope so if he's going to call that late," she said with a mix of fake and real annoyance.

Henry laughed, but just over twenty years of marriage gave him a pretty good idea of what was bothering her. His partner Lexie's absence, coupled with the shut down, had left him with painfully little to do over the past several months. Monica's law firm had still been open and managed to have some jobs for him, but it was all low effort computer-based stuff, netting little pay and having nothing to do with the private investigation agency's more "specialized" work.

The agency hadn't been in great financial shape before, thanks to them losing some lucrative yet unethical work his previous partner had kept from him, but now things were so tight he was worried about keeping the office in Washington Heights. He'd tried to keep giving Martin some nominal pay as he worked through their backlog of digitizing things while at his parents', but there was only so much he could work on without coming into the city, and to Henry's embarrassment he had to stop. Martin had been more than understanding, which made it worse, but Henry had made it up to him by continuing his training while Monica was at work and the kids were at virtual school.

In some ways, the break from the supernatural was a blessing, as the agency had been featured on a conspiracy website, alleging they'd instigated a riot in an affluent Jersey suburb. They'd been partially right, but Henry had gone to great lengths over the years to keep them under the radar. It was a relief the publication had happened just before lockdown and the site, "New Borderlands News," had moved on to medical disinformation and anti-vax nonsense. Not great for their subscribers, but it also moved the spotlight away from the fact the majority of their information had come from a reporter who died under what they called "mysterious circumstances." It wasn't explicitly stating Lexie or

Henry were involved in it, but they had been and their failure to intervene and save him weighed heavily on Henry.

New York City, especially Manhattan, was a dangerous place to be asking questions about the supernatural, and Henry knew first hand the lengths those in that world would go to keep things from the public eye.

Not having to deal with it all had been a relief at first, but now left him feeling aimless and unprepared for when the other shoe would drop. He'd been able to focus on keeping their teenagers on task and from killing each other, but with Monica going back to the office and the kids out of school he felt like he was in a holding pattern waiting for Lexie to return. Her texts had gotten more infrequent than usual, and he was worried the longer she stayed in her northern New York hometown the less likely she was to return. They'd only been working together for a year and a half before she left and, despite a few rough patches, they'd begun to work well together. Martin hadn't been with them for very long, and Henry didn't have the heart to tell him he may not be ready for regular field-work for a long time, if ever.

"Whoa, Dad's actually wearing real clothes!" Their son John strode out of the hallway, grinning at Henry. "You going to the office again?"

"No, just have some work in New Jersey with Martin."

"'Bout time," John said, heading into the kitchen. "I thought you were giving up the monster hunting."

Henry could see Monica tense in his peripheral vision. They'd kept the kids from the nature of his work for as long as they could, and their discovery of it over a year ago had been violent and traumatic. Monica didn't want them to ever have anything to do with it, but with it out in the open and the initial shock worn off, John's curiosity and laissez faire attitude about it had become a constant source of stress for her.

"You know that's not what it is," Henry said.

"I know, I know," John said, coming out of the kitchen with a cup of coffee and a nearly overflowing bowl of cereal. "But it's good, though. I was beginning to think you'd be staying in those sweatpants."

"Not a chance. You know I've got too much style."

John choked on his coffee when he laughed. "Okay, keep telling yourself that."

"And what have *I* been telling you?" Monica said, the tone stopping him before he retreated back to his room to do whatever he did back there.

He groaned, but Monica's raised eyebrow straightened him out. "College applications."

"Yes, please," she said. "We're already behind and I don't want you to miss anything."

"I know," John said. "And I'm on it. Promise."

"Good," she said as John headed back down the hallway. "And wake your sister! I don't care how late she was up on the computer last night." John disappeared around the corner as he gave them a thumbs up.

"As for you," Monica said, standing up and giving Henry a once over. "I want you to be careful out there, okay?"

"I'm always careful," Henry said, giving her a kiss on the cheek.

"We both know that's not true. When are you going to be back?"

"This afternoon. I'll text you," he said, heading out the door

It was a quick walk to the parking garage where he kept the "company car," a school bus yellow '76 Gremlin held together with literal magic. Once at the car, he texted Martin he was on his way, and then put on the 90s hip-hop playlist he'd all but given up on listening to at home thanks to his children's incessant commentary and teasing about it.

Yes Lillian, they should not be using "the gay F-word."

Yes John, "Whomp, there it is" is four words to get busy, not three.

Yes Lillian, Kanye is very problematic.

Yes John, "bump your head and then you wake up in the Dawn of the Dead" sounds like House of Pain is describing The Walking Dead.

Yes Lillian, all women are not bitches.

Yes John, Biz Marquis absolutely was inappropriate to his female employee in "Just A Friend."

He was thankful to have such socially-conscious children, but he'd expected them to turn their gaze to the rest of the world instead of their father, who just wanted to happily enjoy a golden age of music far superior to the one they'd been born into. He turned up the music and then headed for the tunnel, hoping he'd beaten the weekend traffic but resigned to the fact you never could.

***

Martin was waiting for him at a retro looking coffee shop nestled among Cedar Ridge's pricey suburban boutiques that could only exist in a climate of vast disposable income. Martin sat at one of the weirdly shaped plastic booths in the back corner and waved Henry over as soon as he walked in.

"I'm sorry we couldn't meet at my house. My mom is still adjusting to my 'questionable employment choice,' and if she heard us talking shop it would be just...," he just shook his head.

Henry held up his hand. "Believe me, I hear you. You said you got something about that place?"

"Yeah, and let me start by saying if I'd known it was built where it was I wouldn't have gone."

"There's a history?"

"Oh yeah," Martin said, pulling his laptop out of his backpack. "It's the Cedar Ridge Murder House. Where it used to be, I mean."

"Murder House?"

"Not the catchiest name, but neither was 'The Cedar Ridge Slayings,' which is what they called what happened there in the 50s." The laptop opened to a picture of an old front page of the Star-Ledger dominated by a picture of a scrawny and terrified White man looking to be in his late twenties. He was wearing shackles and a prison uniform while being roughly dragged away from a screaming mob of people. The headline read "Justin Corwin Arrested for Cedar Ridge Slayings!" Below, a bit smaller, it read "Community Demands the Death Penalty."

"So Justin here," Martin said, "kidnapped five kids, locked them in his basement, and then tortured and eventually killed all but one of them. Oh, and he offed his parents too."

"Jesus."

"Oh, don't worry, it gets worse. Apparently, he didn't just kill these kids. He dismembered them so he could burn the bodies in his furnace, which was one of those old-timey, coal-fired ones."

"Hence the outrage," Henry said.

"Oh yeah, they wanted him dead real bad. But he didn't even make it to trial before hanging himself in his cell. But here's the potentially interesting part. He said the furnace was instructing him to kill."

"That is interesting."

Martin switched to another tab. "The whole thing kind of got swept under the rug on account of, well...the suburbs. Fast-forward to ten years ago, when disgruntled teen Jackson Cole does a Cedar Ridge Slayings remix to terrorize some other kid. He kills six people, kidnaps that other kid, and they end up at said Murder House. Cops come find them, Cole gets killed, and the house ends up being burned to the ground to no one's dismay."

Henry nodded. "And your friend's family bought the lot it was on and built their own house."

"Acquaintance at best," Martin said. "Murder House 2.0 went up about six years ago, after the whole thing blew over. Surprise, surprise, the original buyers end up selling after only a couple years. For a loss too, if Zillow is to be believed. Turns out Tim's folks got themselves a real good deal on a haunted house."

"Definitely could be a haunting," Henry said, running a hand against his closely cut beard as he skimmed the report on the screen.

"Could be?" Martin said in exasperation. "I may have been getting crunk but there was definitely something there."

"Crunk?" Henry said, raising an eyebrow.

"You know, drunk a--"

"I know what it means. I just don't know why *you're* saying it."

"Right, sorry. But seriously, if it's not a haunting then what?"

"I'm not saying it is or isn't anything. Haunting is a possibility, but haunting spirits don't usually send people out to do errands. And you said the new kid didn't actually live there?"

"Nope," Martin said, checking some facts in another window. "He lived way up on the hill with his Dad, who he killed in his last spree of murders. They figured Cole was using the house as a place to stash all his gear, but it doesn't look like there's any actual evidence of that. Plus, they didn't really get a chance to sweep it for clues afterward."

"Interesting. Was it local PD or the Sheriff's Department handling the case?"

Martin clicked through a few more screens. "It looks like it was locals."

Henry nodded. "Good. They tend to be a little more receptive than Sheriffs. Let's see if we can find who was in charge of the investigation and if they can give us any specifics on what went down."

"I'm excited," Martin said, packing up his laptop. "My first witness interview. And also first interview with the cops." That slowed him down. "First *conversation* with cops, actually."

"Must be nice," Henry smirked as they headed for the door.

"I get that," Martin blushed. "Total privilege move, for sure."

"I'm playing with you. I've been spending too much time with the kids."

"I bet," Martin laughed. "They told me about catching you doing what passed for dancing in the living room."

Henry stopped short. "When the hell did they tell you that?"

"Oh," Martin said, taken aback. "It was in the group chat."

"Of course there's a group chat," Henry muttered. The whole office, plus his family, seemed to have multiple ones and he'd asked to be kept off as many as possible. Clearly that was a mistake.

"You're just lucky there wasn't video. Lily was totally going to try to get some." Henry stopped and glared. "For educational purposes," Martin added. "It sounded like you need better moves."

"You," Henry snapped, "are the last person I'm taking dance advice from. Now dance yourself into this car and navigate us to the police station."

***

"Detective David Prescott? He hasn't worked here in years," the desk sergeant said, looking back down at the screen in front of her.

"You wouldn't happen to have any contact information for him, would you?" Martin asked.

"What am I, a Google?" she said, not looking back up.

"No, of course not," Martin said, looking over his shoulder at Henry, who was standing a few steps behind him. After Martin's initial excitement had been replaced with anxiety, Henry reminded him that this was what came with field work. Resigned, he said he would give it his best. "I'm a writer and I'm, ah, writing a book about the Jackson Cole case and--"

"Sounds fascinating," she said, glaring up at him. "I can't help you. So unless you have other business, I'm going to need you two to step aside."

Martin looked back at him with impending panic and, with a sigh, Henry stepped forward.

"Sergeant, can I have you take a look at this?"

She looked up at Henry, the expression of irritation falling from her face when she saw the silver dollar being flipped across his knuckles. "Now," Henry said, quieter as he stared into her vacant eyes, "can you point us in the direction of someone who knows about the case?"

Her head tilted and her pupils raced back and forth like she was dreaming. "Ronald Lobrazzo, the Chief of Detectives, was involved in the case," she said in a slow, low voice.

"Wonderful," Henry said, hating his satisfaction at how quickly she fell under the charm. "Can you get him for us?"

She nodded slowly, picked up the phone, and dialed an extension.

Martin sidled up next to him. "You did the mind-trick on her?" Henry nodded, not wanting to lose his focus.

The Sergeant hung up the phone and looked back at Henry. "He's on his way," she said, now sounding like she was on the verge of a quiet breakdown. "How else may I serve you?"

"That's new," Martin whispered.

Henry cleared his throat and deposited the coin back into his pocket. The hold on her was slow to fade, and Henry wondered if he could get her to reveal a secret, give her a command for later, or have her--

Knock it the fuck off, he snapped in his head.

The thought receded, leaving him with a sullen twinge of disappointment.

"We'll be over here," Henry said as the Sergeant's eyes refocused. He turned and headed towards a set of chairs in the waiting area.

"I thought that was for emergencies," Martin asked as they sat.

"Well, best not to waste time."

Martin nodded enthusiastically. "I got you," he said.

"It's still dangerous," Henry added, knowing he was setting a bad example. "And not something that should be done often, but since we're on a little bit of a deadline I figured I should grease the wheels some."

"When are you going to teach me that, anyway? It'd come in real handy when my mother goes on one of her 'wasted potential' rants."

"What did I just say? This is why I haven't taught it to you yet." Henry didn't add that it wasn't really something that could be taught.

"Can I help you?" a heavyset White man in a too-small suit and a too-thick graying mustache asked them from the bullpen door.

"Chief Lobrazzo," Henry said, getting up and extending a hand. "So very nice to meet you. My name is Henry Churchill and this is my associate Martin Green. We were hoping to talk to you about the Jackson Cole case."

"We're writing a book," Martin smiled unsteadily.

"Huh," Lobrazzo said, appraising them with narrowed eyes that seemed even smaller under his large forehead and massively unkempt eyebrows as he took Henry's hand. "Shelly," he called over to the Sergeant, "I got it from here." She nodded, a look of confusion on her face as if she hadn't realized the three of them had been there the whole time.

"I figured it was a matter of time," Lobrazzo said as they followed him back to his office. "That case was weird from the jump, and it only got weirder."

"It does seem that way," Henry said.

"Oh yeah," Lobrazzo said, taking a seat behind his desk and motioning for them to sit as well. "I didn't get assigned to it at first, but once it started going off the rails they called me in to straighten it out." He leaned back, a smug "I told you so" edge coming into his voice.

"David Prescott was the lead on it, right?"

Lobrazzo nodded. "Yup. He was all over it. On it way too close, if you ask me. I was the head of the Investigative Unit then and for some reason the Chief let him run with his bullshit theories."

"You don't say," Henry said, relieved that they wouldn't need more magic to get information out of him. "You had a different take on it?"

"I sure fucking did. I mean, there's physical evidence that tied Cole to the murders, but it was that other kid who never sat right with me."

"Who now?" Martin chimed in.

"The other kid, the one he was going after. He was a twitchy little weirdo and, honestly, I always thought he and Cole had a little something going on and that's what the whole thing was about." Lobrazzo waggled his hand in what Henry assumed was an indicator of gayness. "Kid wouldn't talk, though. Probably because Prescott babied him the whole time, and when I stepped in they wouldn't let me really put the full-court press on him."

"That is a shame," Martin chimed in, his nerves having settled a bit. Lobrazzo looked at him, smart enough to realize it could have been insincere, but Martin covered with a smile.

"You said it was weird?" Henry said to refocus Lobrazzo's attention.

"Oh yeah. We never released this but...," Lobrazzo paused, and Henry couldn't tell if it was for dramatic effect or genuine worry at being overheard. "The first murder, victim's place was set on fire. But her? Not a cinder. She was laying on the floor in an unburned circle. Fire said they'd never seen anything like it."

Henry had, but he wasn't going to tell Lobrazzo where.

"The murder weapon itself was something weird as hell too. Like a sword or some long blade that was old, thin, and really fucking sharp according to the lab. Like, where the hell do you get something like that?"

"Sword store?" Martin said. Henry gave him a look that he hoped conveyed that there was relaxed and then there was *too* relaxed.

"We don't have a lot of those," Lobrazzo said, demeanor stiffening again.

"It wasn't recovered?" Henry asked, trying to draw back his attention.

"Nope. We figured it burned up when the place caught fire."

"How did that happen, anyway?" Martin asked.

"That," Lobrazzo said, pointing his finger at him, "is an excellent question, and one I wish I could answer. The only people there were Prescott and two of the kids Cole 'kidnapped.'" The air-quotes were readily apparent. "They said Cole started the furnace because he wanted to, y'know," he made hacking motions with his hand, "but it exploded somehow and then the place just went up like a matchbook."

"So there were two other kids involved, not just one?" Henry asked.

"Yeah. The weirdo and a girl that was seeing him and whose family, by the way, were attacked by Cole. While she wasn't there. At nearly one in the morning." Lobrazzo's significant eyebrows rose with each sentence.

"That wasn't in any of the reports," Martin said, looking pointedly over at Henry.

"Yeah, you know, juveniles and privacy and all that. The timelines for all of them that day were screwy. Probably some kind of sex thing. Usually is, especially with teenagers. Maybe love triangle gone bad, maybe some Satanist stuff on account of the burning and all. But after six murders people wanted to get the whole thing wrapped, so here we are." Lobrazzo threw his hands up in the air.

"That's wild," Henry said, nodding in sympathy. "What about the weird kid? Any follow-up or anything?"

"Nah. Ended up going into the foster system but must have turned out okay. I keep my eyes peeled in case he gets picked up on something. If he does, I'm gonna open this thing up again and really put the screws to him."

"So who is he?" Martin asked. "Maybe we could, y'know, put the screw-gie on him ourselves." He accompanied this by twisting his fist around in a nearly obscene gesture, which seemed to just confuse and irritate Lobrazzo.

He held up a hand to stop whatever it was that Martin was doing. "I'm good, thanks. Like I said, privileged and sealed information. Nothing I can do."

"Aw nuts," Martin huffed in exaggerated dismay. "You sure about that?"

Lobrazzo's brows eclipsed his eyes. "Yeah. I am."

"Well alright then," Henry said, slapping the arms of his chair and getting to his feet. "Chief, you've been a real help." He extended a hand and Lobrazzo stood and shook it.

"My pleasure. And if, by some chance," he looked over at Martin, "you find anything out I'd appreciate knowing about it."

"Of course," Henry nodded. "Always willing to lend a hand to law enforcement."

They made their way out of the building, taking a wide berth around the desk Sergeant, and when they got outside Martin let out a great sigh. "Okay, that was kind of cool."

"Screw-gie?" Henry chuckled, shaking his head.

"Sorry. Seinfeld has been my comfort show."

"I'll give you that. So, Mr. Investigator, what's our next step?"

"Oh, the sister for sure!" Martin was practically skipping. "Nothing said she was there and if she was involved with the other kid she probably knows a lot more. Especially given that this thing is most certainly spooky."

"Got it in one," Henry said, giving him a congratulatory pat on the shoulder.

***

They headed back towards the coffee shop and by the time they got there Martin had found Christine Baker, sister of murder victim number three and daughter of the only attack survivor. She was living in New Mexico, was a sales rep for something that was either an insurance or pharmaceutical company, rented a condo, was in just a bit more debt than the average Millennial, and had no arrests or court cases. Her social media was pretty basic, with a bit of a Southwest-witchy vibe, and was, as Martin put it, "not unattractive."

"I'm going to handle this, if you don't mind." Henry said, putting the phone in the dash holder and putting it on speaker.

"For sure," Martin nodded. "This is definitely not my forte."

It rang twice and then went to voicemail. Martin opened his mouth to say something but Henry held up a hand. "Ms. Baker, my name is Henry Churchill, a detective with the Cedar Ridge Police Department. I wanted to talk to you about some new developments and information regarding the attack on your family a few years back. If you could give me a call back at this number, that'd be great," he said, and then ended the call.

"And now we wait?" Martin asked dubiously.

"I'm willing to bet she'd be interested in hearing about 'new developments,' especially if the story they gave was a cover."

"Or she could be too traumatized and just wants to forget," Martin said. Henry looked over at him. "Okay," he added, "she can be two things."

Henry was about to respond when the phone buzzed, displaying her number.

"Never doubt me, son," Henry said, giving him a wink.

"Is this Ms. Baker?" he asked when he picked up.

"Yeah," came the tentative female voice. "Is this Detective Churchill?"

"Just Henry, please," he said, projecting as much warmth in his voice as he could. "And I've got you on speaker with my associate, Martin."

"Hi," Martin piped up, giving a little wave and then rolling his eyes at himself.

"Hi," she said, her tone clipped and defensive. "You said you had information?"

"We do, but we were hoping we could review your statement with you if you have a moment."

"Fuck's sake, do you think I'm going to remember anything more than I did ten years ago? Just tell me what you've got, I need to get on a meeting in a few minutes."

"There's been another incident," Henry said. "At the Briarcliff house."

"That's not possible," she snapped. "It burned to the ground."

"You saw that first hand, correct?"

There was a pause. "Yeah. And?"

"There's a new house on the property and we have reason to believe that the occupants may be in danger in a way that's related to your case."

"I really doubt that, *Henry*," she said sarcastically. "The person responsible is dead, so whatever it is it has nothing to do with what happened to my family."

"He's dead like, shot through the eye and leaving a big hole in his face dead?" Martin chimed in. That landed an even longer pause.

"Who told you that? Was it Detective Prescott? Was it...Look, it doesn't matter how you know because--"

"Because I saw him," Martin continued. "Saw right through what looked like his very douchey head. It, and he, were deeply unpleasant. Also on fire."

Another pause.

"Ms. Baker," Henry continued slowly, "we know there was a supernatural element to the crimes centered around the Briarcliff house, and I have reason to believe that now it's, for lack of a better term, waking up. We could really use your help to make sure no one else gets hurt like you and your family did."

"Jesus Christ," she whispered. "Jesus fucking Christ." There was another pause. "You aren't actually with the cops, are you Henry?"

"You did catch me in a lie, yes," he said. "But my associate and I handle things like this regularly and this...re-emergence came to our attention. No one has been hurt yet, but in my experience with things like this it's only a matter of time."

There was a long exhale and from the noise on the line it sounded like she'd started walking. "Shit, shit, shit!" Another long breath. "Have you talked to Mark? Mark Watson, I mean."

"I take it he's the boy Cole was stalking," Henry said. "They kept his name, and yours, under wraps since you were minors."

"Thank God for small favors. Okay, I can send you the info I have and you can probably find him. He's still in Jersey."

"That's helpful," Martin muttered.

"I have to go into a meeting, like, now so I don't have the time to get into it, but he knows all about this. In the...supernatural sense, I mean."

"Got it," Henry said. "Send us what you have and we'll take it from there."

***

What she had was just a neglected Facebook page, but it plus what Lobrazzo had told them was enough to run a search. He was renting a condo in West Orange and worked at Clairidge Collision & Auto, also in West Orange. His credit was decent, he owned a '79 Jeep, and like Lobrazzo had said, kept himself on the right side of the law (aside from a few speeding tickets). Henry decided in this case, and because West Orange was so close, they should try him in person and headed to his job.

The garage was a very polished non-chain or dealer-owned one, and looked to service mostly high-end luxury and classic cars. When they asked after Mark the receptionist nodded and paged him over the intercom. After a few moments he emerged from the swinging doors across the lobby.

"Can I help you guys?" he said. He was of average height and in good shape, just-barely shaved, and his hair was close-cropped on the sides with the length on top slicked back. He rubbed his dirty

35

hands on his equally dirty overalls as he looked them over, trying to place where he might know the two of them from.

"I'm Henry Churchill, Mr. Watson. I'm a private investigator and--"

"Shit," he muttered, immediately dropping his customer service mask. "Is this about Ashley? Because I told her plenty of times it was over and I'm not going to couples counseling with a girl I dated for two months."

"Oh yeah, don't do that," Martin said, shocked. "But this isn't about that, thank god. I'm Martin, by the way."

"Okay," Mark said warily, appraising them cautiously. "So what can I do for you guys? We're kind of slammed today."

"Is there somewhere we can talk privately?" Henry asked.

"Not until I know what this is about," he said, smiling in a most unfriendly way.

"It's...," Henry shifted, turning away from the receptionist and lowering his voice so he couldn't be heard from across the room, "about the house on Briarcliff Avenue."

Everything in Mark's body seemed to shut down for a second, and then rebooted as a block of steel. "What the fuck is this?" he said through a clenched jaw. "Is this some kind of *Investigate the Unknown* bullshit?"

"No, not at all," Henry said in a well-practiced, 'talking calmly to an upset white man' voice. "I handle cases of this nature and I got your name from Christine Baker."

"Huh," he said, his tension easing for a moment but returning just as fast. "Look, I'm not talking about that shit, so you guys are just wasting your time. Tell Christine I said hey, and good luck with whatever."

"It's back," Martin said, a little too loudly as Mark turned away.

Mark snapped around and gave Martin a death glare. "Keep your fucking voice down," Mark hissed, and then registered what Martin said. "And that's bullshit. I saw him...it, whatever the fuck it was, burn and die. Or however that works. If there's something else then it has nothing to do with me."

"It's not that easy, Mr. Watson," Henry said. "We just want to talk about what you experienced so we know what we're dealing with and can protect the people who live there now."

"People *live* there? Of course they fucking do, it's the suburbs." Mark closed his eyes and took a few deep breaths and a fraction of the tension in his body faded. "That sucks for them, but I'm not going to be a part of this. It wasn't my fault, and that shit is in the past. The way past."

"I understand that what happened to you was traumatic," Henry said. "But the more I know the more we can--"

"If you think I have any insight into what happened then you're mistaken." Mark let out another breath and Henry could feel the adrenaline pouring off of him. Mark took a step back and then said, loud enough for the receptionist to hear, "I'm sorry, I can't help you guys. Best of luck to you."

Before Henry could say anything the man spun on his heel and disappeared behind the doors he came from.

"Well alrighty then," Martin said as they walked back to the car. "What now? We're not going to have to, like, pester him or something, are we? Because he seemed...intense."

"We'll give him some time to cool off," Henry said. "We did just drop in to casually talk about the worst thing that's ever happened to him."

"Good point," Martin said. "But how long do we give it?"

"Until we've exhausted the rest of our options."

Chapter Three

Options were exhausted in a little over a week, although for a couple of days Henry took a break for paying (thank god) PI work. They'd reconnected with Christine a couple of days later and she'd given them a pretty brief overview of what Mark had told her after the Briarcliff house burned down. The official story was, as Henry had known, mostly bullshit. It'd been Mark, not Jack (as Jackson was known) who committed the murders, but while being controlled by what she helpfully called "a darkness ghost of some kind." Mark said he'd dreamed about what happened at the house in the fifties, seeing it through the eyes of one of Corwin's victims, but also the murders being committed in the present (the mystery murder weapon being a sword-cane, of all things). The "darkness ghost" was tied to the furnace of the house and ended up reanimating Jack's corpse after he'd been killed.

It was clear why they came up with something else, but what was irritatingly not clear was what the entity in the house really was. It could be a "cursed land" situation, but if that had been the case it'd have made its presence known before the Corwins lived there. A house haunting was also unlikely, as those tend to end when the structure is destroyed. Even if it was a haunting, it would have been unheard of for it to reach across town and latch itself onto a random teenager that'd never noticed the place before.

There had to be some kind of connection between Mark and the house, but she told him that the only thing Mark came up with was that he'd been connected somehow to the kid he'd been dreaming about. Henry's bullshit detector had pinged a little bit on that, so he and Martin started looking through birth records and family histories both in the fifties and when Mark was born, but there was no connection. The boy Mark had been dreaming of was Corwin's final victim, Darren Cox, who was also the only survivor of the kidnappings. Cox had an unremarkable life after that, never married or had children, and ended up purchasing the Briarcliff house and ultimately killing himself there shortly after. Tragic, and a definite suspect for a haunting presence, but that would have been after Corwin's supernatural encounter.

There was a piece they were missing, and it was the one that would tell them what kind of magic or ritual was needed to put whatever it was down for good. Martin had walked by the house daily over the course of the week, and he said that now that he was looking for it he could feel the same undercurrent of malevolence he'd experienced before. On the pass he'd made earlier that day he said he smelled smoke outside, and when he paused to look closer he'd seen Jack's burned and one-eyed presence waving at him from a window.

It hadn't just woken up. It was getting stronger.

Henry told him to hold off on any more walk-bys in case it was feeding off of Martin's presence and magical acumen. They'd called and left messages for Mark until they both were blocked, so he called Christine again. He'd been avoiding doing so as she'd requested, but she couldn't remember anything specific Mark had said about the rituals Corwin was performing. Her response was emphasized with the sharpest of "fuck off" tones, and when he asked if it was possible for her to reach out and talk to Mark she hung up on him.

He could just let the whole thing go, but the mystery of it was something his brain needed to pick at, not to mention what could potentially happen if things got worse there. If the rituals Corwin had been performing had cracked open some kind of gate or managed to summon something, then things were going to get a lot worse a lot faster.

"Hey Dad."

Henry looked up from the book he hadn't really been reading as John dropped onto the sofa. In a lot of ways, John was the kind of teenager Henry had wished he'd been: confident, athletic, tall, and with a clear idea of his future. Even better, he'd gone to diverse and private schools, giving him an opportunity to be around other kids of color, something the Westchester suburb Henry had grown up in had been sorely lacking.

"What's up, my dude," he said, immediately cringing at his attempt at being "with it."

He could tell John wanted to get on his case about it, but instead he looked around the room and started to fidget.

"Uh, you know when Mom's getting home?"

Henry closed the copy of *Ancient Infernal Summoning Rites* in his lap and straightened up his recliner. John's tone suggested this was about a different kind of horror, one deeper and more existential. "She's working late. What's up?"

"Lily's gaming so I just was hoping we could talk without them around."

"Okay," he said, trying not to start fidgeting himself. "Speak your mind."

"It's about...you know..." He gestured to the book on Henry's lap, as well as the other ones stacked on the table next to him. Henry held back a sigh of relief at this not being a more personal and life-changing teenage boy emergency, but chided himself for getting too comfortable and thinking he could do research in the living room and not have it be an issue.

"Oh," Henry said. "What about it?"

"I know Mom doesn't really like it, so I get why we don't talk about it any more but..." John trailed off. When the secret was out and they'd answered the kids' questions, it was made clear that it was never to be discussed anywhere but home, but as more questions continued to come up it was made readily apparent that talk even at home put Monica on edge, so conversation ceased. John's comment when Henry had gone out to Jersey had been the first one in nearly a year.

They hadn't told the kids she hadn't found out about this until after they were married, or that it was part of the darkest part of their marriage and had almost split them up. After things had worked out as best they could, she accepted Henry was making it part of his work life, but made it clear she wanted nothing to do with it. When she was pregnant with John she told him she didn't ever want their kids involved either, something he was more than happy to agree with.

"I'm happy to answer anything, but for a lot of reasons the less you know the better. I told you how dangerous it is."

"I get that," John said with exasperation. "I just..."

Before Henry could interject he started up again. "Why are you teaching Martin to do more magic if that's the case?"

That was unexpected, and Henry leaned back as he gathered his thoughts.

"When did he tell you that?" he asked, buying himself some time to come up with an answer.

"We text and junk," John said a little sheepishly.

"Mmm-hmm." That goddamn group chat again. "And what did he tell you?"

"Just that he was learning new stuff while he was out there. But he also said I should talk to you if I had more questions."

"That's good," he said, relieved that Martin had enough common sense for that at least. "The thing is, Martin had already used magic when Lexie and I met him, and he experienced the consequences of messing with it. He's well aware of the risks, and doesn't want anything like that to happen again. Plus, teaching him some stuff is helpful when we need a few more hands on deck on a case."

"Because not everyone can actually do it."

"Exactly. Like Lexie, who is one of the least talented I've ever seen. Just absolutely terrible, and not just with her pronunciation," he laughed, but failed to lighten the mood.

"So why teach him more, especially if it puts him in danger?"

Henry hesitated. "It was his choice. He was having a hard time after what happened and it's helped him feel more in control and secure." John raised an eyebrow at that. "Okay, slightly more secure."

"But having someone else around who can do magic is helpful."

"Right."

"So, by that logic, you should have as many people who can do magic helping you as possible, right?"

Boy, did it suck to have a kid that's smarter than you, and especially one that was on the debate team. "I see what you're doing, and I'm going to stop you right there," Henry said, sitting back up and pointing at him for emphasis. "This is not up for discussion. You are never--"

"Really?" John snapped. "*Never*? Is it that obvious that I can't do it?"

Henry took a breath.

"It's not about that. I don't know if you've got the talent or not and I don't want to know. You shouldn't either. Like I said, it's *dangerous*."

"I know, I know. But Martin says that it runs in families, so it's a possibility, right?"

Henry shook his head. "That's never been proven. No one else in my family can do it, so there's no proof you'd to be able to."

"How do you know? You said you figured out by accident, and so did Martin. Maybe everyone else just never had a chance to find out. Can't you at least do some kind of test or whatever on me? Or did you already do one and you don't want to tell me about it?"

Henry ran a hand across the top of his head, hoping it'd help him formulate some kind of strategy. "Here's the thing," Henry said, leaning closer for emphasis. "Magic has a cost. Sometimes it's obvious, sometimes it's not. What I'm teaching Martin is basic, mostly harmless stuff or things to keep him safe that don't take as much of a toll on you. Anything more, you get into taking years off your life, permanently damaging your health, and even your soul. I've explained this to him so he can figure out what he wants to stay away from. Not to mention the fact he's an adult."

John rolled his eyes. "So in like, two years, I can try? That doesn't make any sense!"

"In *no* amount of years can you try," Henry said. "This is not for you."

John exhaled sharply, looking down at his feet. "I just don't get why you're willing to teach...some guy and not me. What if you need someone else to get your back?"

Henry got up from the recliner and sat on the couch next to him so he could put a hand on John's shoulder. "I am never, ever, going to put you in harms way. So the magic stuff is never going to happen, okay?" John slumped, hearing the finality in Henry's voice.

"But what if...what if Mom or Lillian need it and you're not around? If I've got to protect them...what can I do?" Henry pulled him into an awkward, one armed embrace. The kids had been spared the worst of the attack that let the magical cat out of the bag, and Henry had tried not to think about the lasting and non-magical toll it had taken on them.

"Hey, it is not your job to protect this family. That's on me, and I'm sorry I couldn't do a better job of it, but nothing like that is going to happen again."

John looked at him skeptically. "You don't know that for sure."

"Okay, you're right, but I can tell you that the more involved you get in this, the more likely something *is* going to happen." John looked dubious at that, and Henry continued before he could interrupt. "Knowing about this has made things very difficult over the years. If I'd have left it alone, these kinds of things would never happen at all. And over the past twenty-five years I've seen things that people should not see, and done things and made choices that I'm not proud of. I couldn't live with myself if you had to experience anything like that."

"Is that why you didn't tell us how it all got started?"

"Yeah," Henry said. "It was horrible and not something you need to worry about." John looked like he was going to argue but then stopped himself.

"And you don't have to worry about backing me up. I back *you* up, okay? Your Dad's the big dog, remember? He can take care of himself. Sometimes you just need an extra set of hands for stuff, and that's where Martin comes in. You're still my favorite son, after all."

"Yeah, yeah," John rolled his eyes, having heard that corny joke ever since Lillian was born, and slid his way out of the embrace with a chuckle that could have been genuine.

"You've got too much going on for you to carry this weight. Let it go, focus on school and the college search. By the way, ha—"

"No, I haven't finished with that pile Mom gave me."

"Please get to it, she doesn't need to be stressing either."

"I know, I know." Shoulders slumped, John turned back to the hall.

"Hey," Henry called after him. "We good?"

John gave him a weak smile over his shoulder and said "We good" just before he disappeared around the corner.

Henry leaned back and let out a deep sigh. He'd known something had been off with him these past few months, but Henry had stupidly attributed it to the horrors of the real world taking its toll. He'd been too focused on those things as well, but he knew he'd have to do a better job of making sure they were okay. The upside was that while his son may be smarter than him, but he couldn't spot a lie like his old man could.

***

The next day, feeling like he had no other option, Henry followed Mark home from work. He knew where he lived, but the casual suburban pursuit was also a good way to see if the charm he'd placed on the Gremlin would, in fact, keep him from being consciously noticed. Given that he'd been able to pull into the spot next to Mark's without him giving Henry more than a glance was definitely a good sign. Henry followed Mark through the maze of upscale condos from a good distance and rounded the corner as Mark was stepping through his door.

"Mr. Watson," Henry called, closing the distance between them in a quick stride. "I need to talk to you."

Mark's confusion lasted a second, and it was enough for Henry to put his foot against the door.

"What the fuck, man?" Mark said, tossing the keys and handful of mail onto a table. "I told you I don't want anything to do with this shit."

"I know, but this is important. Lives are at stake."

"I don't *care*," Mark said, leaning against the door to get it to close but unable to budge Henry's foot. "Look, I don't like the optics of it, but I *will* call the cops, okay?"

"Mr. Watson, whatever made you kill those people is waking back up, and I need to stop it." He didn't want to swing the biggest club he had, but Mark looked frustrated enough to follow up on the threat.

Mark took a step back, gasping. "Fuck," he muttered, his voice sounding like it would've in high school. "Fuck you, that's not..." His face went red, and Henry raised his hand to calm him down.

"I know you didn't. Christine told us everything, okay, and it's not your fault. I'm not blaming you."

Mark's expression rolled back a click from "impending meltdown" to "confused fury" and he shook his head. "Fucking Christine. Great, so you know everything, that should be more than enough for you to fix it, right?"

"No, not right," Henry said. "There are too many variables, and if I try the wrong thing it could make it a whole lot worse."

"Then that's a real big problem for someone else," Mark said.

The coin was out of his pocket before he could reasonably claim he'd thought about it. He danced it along his fingers and it caught Mark's eyes immediately, slipping him into a trance state at the same faster than normal speed the desk Sergeant had before. He didn't want it to come to this, but it was clear this was the only way Henry was going to be able to find out what Mark knew, and the growing danger outweighed the right to privacy.

Yes, keep telling yourself that.

Henry refocused on Mark's mind, but before he could get a command out there was a push from somewhere inside Mark's head that broke the connection. Mark snapped back to reality, looked confused for a few seconds, and then remembered Henry's presence.

"Look. Enough is fucking enough, okay? Please don't make me physically get you off my doorstep," he said, looking Henry up and down. "You don't look like you're in great shape and I really don't want to hurt anybody."

Henry backed up. There were other ways to proceed but they were much more invasive, and Henry knew he'd been through enough and didn't deserve that. Even with the looming danger hanging over them. "I got it. I'm going, Mr. Watson."

"Stop fucking calling me that," he said, following Henry as he backed out of the doorway. "Mr. Watson is my dead dad."

The door slammed.

Henry walked back to the car, dropping the coin he was still clutching into his pocket. It hadn't felt like Mark had pushed him out of his mind consciously, but something was in there that didn't want Henry poking around, most likely part of his previous encounter. It created a new wrinkle to the problem as well, since it might affect him like it had before. Without knowing what caused it in the first place, Henry wouldn't be able to protect him even if Mark wanted to cooperate. Henry thought again about how he could force the issue and what he could do to mitigate whatever side effects there might be, but he shook those thoughts off.

"That's a last resort," he said to himself.

Henry drove off and pulled into the next gas station he saw. There were no good options left, so even though he told Christine he wouldn't call again he figured he'd bend the promise by texting her. An idea came to him as he was wondering what to send to her, and even though he didn't really like it, he typed out the message, muttered to himself, and then hit send.

Chapter Four

"Come on-a my house, my house-a come on..."

That fucking song was stuck in Mark's head the rest of that day, even after he smoked himself halfway to oblivion that night. He hadn't thought about it, Briarcliff, or anything Cedar Ridge in years and entirely by design. He'd been able to hold them at bay for a decade that guy and his nerdy sidekick had been pestering him, but the surprise visit must have been the last straw for his formidable powers of denial. He spent most of his mental energy working on tricks various therapists had given him when he was triggered, but none of them helped.

He wasn't just triggered, he was detonated.

The only remote positive was the mention of Christine. It was hard to shove her into the box with the rest of that shit, but it felt stupidly nostalgic and comforting to think about their brief relationship. He remembered being told by Therapist Number

Three he shouldn't be so fixated on the past, and tried to push those thoughts and the memories of Cedar Ridge as deep as possible.

It's not your problem anymore.

He was on the afternoon shift that day, and after he clocked in Bethany stuck her head in the break room to call him over. "There's someone waiting for you," she said.

"Why wouldn't there be?" he smirked, covering for the sudden panic. If it was Churchill again he knew he was going to wind up on the internet as another crazy guy yelling at a Black dude, which would probably lead to people finding out why Churchill was there, and then everything would be opened up for everyone to know and to stare at him and everyone else would find out who he really was and then--

"Shut up," he growled under his breath as he headed to the front. This was catastrophising and spiraling out over nothing, he told himself. In the words of his Therapist Number Two, that was "negative self-talk" and he should "say it isn't welcome here." Take a breath. Clear your head. He stopped at the door leading out to the waiting area, did just that, and then stepped out.

See, you were crazy thinking this had anything to do with all that stuff! Anyway, look who's here!

It wasn't Churchill, so that was great, but when he saw the shoulder-length, light red hair of the slender woman sitting in the customer lounge scrolling through her phone with Starbucks cups on the table next to her, he recognized her immediately. Even after ten years.

Christine *fucking* Baker. Not 48 hours after he'd been ambushed in his own home, here she was for the first time in a decade from all the way across the country.

Wasn't this what you were hoping would happen when you were scrolling through her Instagram the other night?

He tried to remember the reasons he should be mad at her, even though they were ancient history, but then she looked up at him and smiled. She looked mostly the same, nearly his height and dressed in a relaxed-yet-expensive way. The only obvious change he could see was a black-and-white tattoo of twisting ivy descending from under her short right sleeve and ending just above her elbow. On her wrist he could see a smaller one that seemed to be a pair of dates with an infinity symbol underneath.

"What the hell," was all he could come up with to say by the time he reached her. Some things never changed.

"Hello to you too," she said, giving him a hug. His breath hitched for a moment and then he returned the embrace. He held the hug longer than he should've, but not as long as he wanted.

"What are you doing here?" he asked.

She tilted her head a little at that. "I think you know why I'm here. But I'm also fighting jet-lag from the late flight and I'm still two hours behind. Can we talk somewhere?"

At least someone understands privacy.

Mark shrugged. "Yeah, sure...but I just got in. Can it wait?"

She raised an eyebrow. "Really?"

"It's busy today," he said, not adding that it was busy every day. "But I'm only here for a few hours. Can it wait that long?"

"Sure," she said, despite the fact she obviously didn't think so.

"There's wi-fi," he said, pointing at the ceiling for some reason. "And I can get them to change the TV to whatever you want."

"Look at you," she snickered. "Wielding so much power."

"I'm very good at what I do," he said, cheeks blushing.

"Then do it quickly," she said, pointing at the service bay doors behind him.

"I'll do my best, I promise," he said, backing up and not looking away from her until he absolutely had to.

***

It was amazing how fast work could get done given the right incentive. After closing his tickets a half hour faster than he'd expected, he spent the rest of the time in the restroom, scrubbing hands like he was a surgeon and being thankful he kept extra pomade and deodorant in his locker. He stopped at the door to the lounge, did some of his breathing exercises, and then headed in.

"I went as fast as I could," he said, arms raised in apology.

"It's fine," she said, nodding towards the two late middle aged women with impeccably coiffed hairdos behind the reception counter. "Tracy and Jeanette kept me entertained."

"Those two," Mark smiled, jabbing a finger at them as they walked past, "are not to be trusted. Especially Jeanette!" The two women giggled and waved at them as they left and headed around to the parking lot.

"They were very interested to hear what you were like in high school, by the way," Christine said, giving him a knowing glance.

"Oh Jesus," he said, rolling his eyes. "I can only imagine the shit they'll give me over it, so thanks for that. Do I even want to know what you said?"

"Well, they were very interested in the idea of you with long hair and, for some reason, they seemed very surprised that you weren't...how did Jeanette put it? Oh yeah, a 'smooth-talking Casanova back then.'"

"Fucking hell," he said, unable to keep from smiling. He paused and then added, "You didn't tell them why you were here, right?"

"Of course not," she said. "I said I was here on a work trip and surprising you. Just being impulsive since the world was closed for so long."

"For sure," he said. "I'm guessing you made it through okay?"

"As well as anyone, I guess," she shrugged. "I started working from home and still am, so that was something." She stopped when Mark did, eyeing his car suspiciously. "This is you?"

"Indeed," he said, giving the cherry red Jeep a pat. "1979 Jeep Cherokee Chief, fully restored."

"I know," she said, pointing at the door. "It says it right there. Is that in case you forget?"

"Very funny," he said, unlocking her door and then going around to the driver's side.

"They also have a thing where you can unlock it remotely, too."

"I'll have you know," he said, once inside, "this is a classic. But that is on the list of things to add."

"I should've figured that you'd end up being a car guy," she said, side-eyeing him with a smile.

"I do pretty okay as a car-guy," he said.

They both paused, the weird giddiness of reconnecting fading and the impending doom of the real reason for her visit looming large.

"Do you want to get something to eat? I know there's not much in the vending machines."

"No shit," she said. "And I don't want to talk about stuff on an empty stomach."

"I know a good place right around here," he said, pulling out of the lot.

"I bet you do," she smirked.

***

He drove them to Panucci's for a late dinner, and after being seated they ordered drinks (white wine for her, Coke Zero for him), and did his best to look like he was actually reading the menu so the conversation hanging over their heads was delayed as much as possible.

"They have a great Alfredo here," he said, putting his menu down.

"Oh, I'm sure you'd know," she winked at him over hers.

"What's that supposed to mean?"

She put her menu down as well. "You're telling me this isn't where you bring all the ladies you're try to woo?"

"Not at all," he said, not volunteering that this was a go-to second-date spot for the pre-wooed. "And who said this was a date?"

"Touche," she said. "I guess I'm still surprised that Mark Watson grew up to be such a player."

"I think you mean 'smooth-talking Casanova,'" he said. "And I'm not. I'll have you know that according to my therapist I have attachment and abandonment issues, so if I were such a thing it wouldn't be my fault."

"A man who goes to therapy," she said in a playfully shocked tone. "Definitely not the kind of thing one expects from a car guy."

"Jesus, why the fuck wouldn't I be in therapy?" he laughed.

"Fair point," she said. "My longest relationship has been with my therapist."

"I somehow feel both happy and sad for you."

"Same, honestly." She took a drink. "So do you want to talk about why I'm here?"

"Abso-fucking-lutely not," he said with a smile. "I'd like to have a good time tonight, not re-live that nightmare. You can't possibly be eager to do so yourself."

"Most of the time. And that's fine, we don't have to do it now, but we need to talk about it at some point, okay? It's important." She stared at him intently.

"Sure," he said. "But for now, tell me about your life."

***

As they waited for their food, she gave him the short version. She finished high school in Connecticut, where they'd moved after Briarcliff so her Aunt could help them recover, and after years of physical therapy her father could walk again. Slowly, and not for long periods of time, but it was something he was still getting better at. Her mother had thrown herself into taking care of him, and once he was mobile again she latched on to local and on-line communities for mothers who'd lost a child "to violence." Christine provided the quotes herself.

"I get it, I guess," she said. "But it feels like she wears what happened like a badge of honor. If I had a nickel for every time she referred to herself as 'a mother who lost a son,' we'd be rich again." The medical and therapy bills, coupled with her father's inability to work, had made a sizable dent in their finances. After college (Northwestern) she moved to Albuquerque for work, which was in "business intelligence" for a company that "provided insurance solutions in the light industrial and benefits field." Mark didn't know what any of that meant but was too afraid to ask.

"So what about you," she asked, finishing her second glass of wine. "I'll confess that I've looked but you're a hard man to Google."

"By design," he said. "But it was okay. Y'know, after. I was only in the system for a couple of years, and the family I ended up with, Rashawn and Amy, are great." He left out how not great the first few were, or how even less great life in a Newark group home had been. "Until they moved away, I would see David, y'know, Detective Prescott, and his family pretty regularly." It was a generous use of "regularly", and he left out how after the move they'd messaged several times and he'd essentially ghosted them.

"Another Coke, hon?" the waitress asked, appearing at his elbow.

"Sure," he said.

"You sure you don't want anything stronger," Christine said after she left. "Given our impending conversation?"

"I have other vices," Mark winked. "Besides, when you grow up with someone who abused alcohol you tend not to have good associations with it."

"Oh," she said, putting down her glass. "That makes sense. I'm sorry, I wasn't thinking. I could get something else if you--"

"It's fine," Mark interrupted. "I'm past being bothered by other people drinking."

"Good," she said, watching the waitress come back with his drink. "Because I'm going to need at least one more."

***

One more turned into two, which she said was just enough to make things fun.

Mark held his tongue as a flurry of sly responses rushed through his brain.

After dessert, they headed out to his car. "Where to?" he asked. "I'm assuming you got a hotel somewhere?"

"Yeah," she said. "And it sucks. Do you live around here?"

"I do indeed," he said, keeping his tone neutral.

"Then let's go there and get on with it."

Once again, Mark made a supreme effort in keeping his mouth shut.

She can't just keep teeing you up like this without an ulterior motive, right?

He drove them to his "surprisingly spacious" condo, as Christine put it. He was relieved he'd left the place almost clean, but made a mental note to not let her go in the kitchen on account of the dishes in the sink.

"Just you then?" she asked.

"Oh yeah," he said. "After growing up in close quarters and in small spaces, I can't live that roommate life." He waited a moment and then asked "What about you?"

"No, thank god, but my place is much smaller," she said, taking in the living room and its plain white walls sparingly decorated with framed monster and kung-fu movie posters, a scarcity of actual furniture, and his impressive wall of fancy electronics.

"I do some custom restoration work on the side," he said as she moved from the living room to the dining area that Mark used as a library and display area for various statues, models, and toys.

"You weren't kidding about the other vices," she said, waving at the nerdy miscellany and ending at the shelves that held bongs and dab rigs.

"I'll remind you that I have PTSD and those are purely for medical use."

"Smart," she said. "I should look into that. And also becoming a mechanic, apparently."

"It has its perks," he said, feeling the rush of pride and confidence he got when thinking about the stability and security it'd finally brought into his life. "We kept busy during lockdown too, so that was something."

"I'm glad you're doing something that you enjoy," she said, a bit of wistful envy in her voice.

"That's a bonus," he said, steering them back to the living room. "A lot of the time working on stuff is the only way life makes sense. Plus, I'm decent enough with computers to handle all the electronic shit they keep putting in cars now. And I got to do it without having student loans hanging over my head, so I've got that going for me."

"Fuck you and your happy life," she sneered, and then took a deep breath. "So are we going to get to it or what?"

"I mean, I still have a lot of cool shit going on in my life we can talk about."

"Whatever," she said, walking back to the living room "Get me something to drink, if you have any booze. Judging by the smell, I don't want to go rooting around in your kitchen."

"I think I might have something," he said, blushing.

He went to the fridge and, remembering her choice at dinner, poured her a glass of white wine from one of the two boxes he kept in his fridge for company. As he passed through the library, he grabbed his humidor but decided not to bring any glassware. Christine was meandering around the living room and looking through her phone. "Here you go," he said. "And if you'd like to partake, I'm happy to provide for you," nodding down at the humidor.

"What a gentleman," she said. "If that's what it's going to take for us to talk then sure. In the meantime, give me your WiFi so we can have some ambiance." He gave her the info and rolled them a joint while she looked through her music app for something "suitable."

"Oh, this is perfect for reliving the past," she snickered after a few moments. As Mark sealed the joint his sound system came to life, blaring auto-tuned guitar riffs through the room before Timbaland asked what somebody like them was doing in a place like this.

"Jesus Christ," Mark said, taking a hit. "I forgot about this song, and for good reason."

"I can't tell you how many parties I heard this at," she said, tossing her phone onto the couch and taking the proffered joint. She inhaled deep and coughed immediately. "Speaking of high school parties," she said. "It's been forever since I smoked." She handed it back to him and started swaying in place. By the time Katy Perry started singing in the background and the tempo picked up, she was dancing with abandon.

"Come on," she said, beckoning him to join her. "Let's have some fun while we can."

"We can have fun for as long as you want," he said, leaning back, "Right now, I'm just going to enjoy the show."

She rolled her eyes, grabbed his hand and pulled him onto his feet, barely giving him a chance to put the joint down. "Don't be a creep." She drew him in close and took hold of his other hand to get him moving.

"I am not great at this," he said, trying to keep up.

"You're fine," she said. The song slowed and she moved closer, mouthing along as Katy took over the vocals. *"Baby tell me, what's your story, I ain't shy, don't you worry,"* she sang along, holding him with her gaze. He raised an eyebrow at the next line where Katy confessed to flirting (with her eye, no less), and that she wanted to leave with him tonight.

"You already did," he said, discovering that dancing and trying to be witty at the same time was beyond him. She looked away, hopping up and down as the chorus resumed. He joined in and they both started scream-singing along to the chorus .

"I'll nev-er be the saaaaa-aame, if we ever meet again. Wooooo-n't let you get awaaaaa-ay, if we ever meet again."

The tempo slowed again and she let go of his hands, putting her arms around his neck and pulling herself close. As they swayed in place, Katy and Timbaland asked to be kissed all night and never let go, and they figured they'd give it a try.

***

'All night' turned out to be 'a solid 45 minutes.' "Respectfully," he said, "That was a horrible time."

"Excuse me?" she said, raising her head off of his chest to glare at him.

"For music," he laughed, taking another hit from the joint that he'd retrieved from the living room, where he'd also turned off the "Hit Songs of 2010" playlist that had been in the background the entire time they'd been otherwise occupied. Not the best ambiance, but at least he could now say that he'd gotten head while listening to 'All I Do Is Win,' which he figured was on someone somewhere's sexual Bingo card.

"Sorry, the first part of that train of thought was in my head."

"Fucking stoner," she said, taking the joint for herself. "Who would of thought the incredibly delicate young man I dated in high school would turn out to be a pothead car guy. Who also fucks pretty good, turns out."

"I contain multitudes," he deadpanned. "But also...'pretty good?' I give a five-star experience, miss. You clearly haven't read my reviews."

"It was more like two, two and a half," she winked, reaching over him to put the joint in the overflowing ashtray on his bedside table. "Maybe if you'd been able to hang on for a *little* bit longer it would've been three."

"Challenge accepted," he said, rolling her onto her back.

"Mark," she said, a hand up to stop him. "I promise I didn't fuck you so we could talk about what's going on, but we absolutely have to."

"And now is the perfect time, sure," he said sourly, extricating himself from her.

"Mark, come on," she said. "You can't just ignore this."

"I have Avoidant Personality Disorder, so I assure you I can." He stood up and looked for some underwear, deciding that if he was going to talk about when a bunch of people they were close to got murdered he wasn't going to do it with his dick out.

"The only reason that I'm here is that the PI guy told me you could be in danger. Just like last time," she said, sitting up.

"How in the hell would he know that?" It suddenly felt like a fist was squeezing his heart.

"They deal with this stuff for a living, and while that may be totally insane I'm going to assume that he knows what he's talking about. Not to mention how they described how Jack died, something no one else knows about."

Just think, you could have another type of reunion as well.

"All the more reason to stay the fuck away. Even if it is true." He had to concentrate on keeping his hands steady so he could zip and button his pants.

"What about the people that live there now? And what if that thing finds a way to get out? Do you think you, or anyone else, will be safe?"

"We will spread His fire across this town, across the world, and nothing will be able to stop us."

"Fuck's sake," he said, trying to get the memory of what the thing had told him out of his head. "If anything, I should stay the hell away from there. He...or it, whatever the fuck, was trying to get me, specifically, and I'm not going to just hand myself over and let it use me again."

"Then just talk to them! Tell him what I don't know so this thing can actually be over. It's just a conversation! Then at least they can get off my ass." She moved to the edge of the bed, looking for her own underwear.

"I'm so sorry you were inconvenienced," he sneered. "By all means, let me open about the worst thing that happened to me and the horrible things I did so you can be more comfortable. Also, I wouldn't even be in this position if you hadn't given them my fucking name. So thanks for that!"

"This is hard for me too, Mark. You're not the only person who went through it."

"Yeah, but I'm the only person who...no fuck this" he snapped, throwing on a t-shirt. "This was great and all, but I have work in the morning and I'm not going to stay up all night arguing." He picked her bra up and tossed it on the bed.

"Wow," she said, drawing the word out to be as reproachful as possible. "You really *are* good at this. I haven't heard 'I have to get up early' in years. Is that part of the five-star experience? Do I get a little gift bag too?"

"Go fuck yourself," he said, leaving the room so she could get dressed.

He was tidying up his humidor when she came back to the living room. "That's what I like about you, Mark," she said. "You're always *almost* a nice guy. I should've picked up on your total fuckboy vibes from the start."

Not the first time you've heard that, is it champ?

"Don't forget your phone," he said, picking it up.

The screen woke as he touched it and he glanced down at her notifications. Something jumped out at him and he jerked the phone away before she could take it. It was a quick read, and when he was done he tossed the phone at her with a derisive laugh.

"Some people really don't change. You forgot to check in with Travis, by the way. He loves and misses you."

Her fair complexion made her blush even more pronounced. "Fuck you," she said, shoving the phone into her purse. "You're not the only one with attachment issues, you know."

"Well, I guess your problem, as usual, is too many attachments," he said, self-righteousness permitting him to look at her now.

She scowled, and he knew she was embarrassed she'd lost the precious moral high ground. "Talk to those guys, don't talk to them, who gives a shit? I figured, given the chance, you'd want to be a grown up about it. Then again, you were always happy to let other people die as long as it meant you didn't have to take responsibility for anything."

He looked down at the large joint he was rolling so he didn't have to watch her storm out and slam the door.

But is she wrong, though? Is she?

Chapter Five

"You said it didn't go great?" the Kid asked.

Christine sloshed the ice in her Starbucks and took another sip. Thanks to last night's onslaught of booze, weed, and terrible decisions she couldn't remember either of their names. She wasn't sure why she thought of the younger one as Kid, as they looked close in age, but the "kid in class who was too excited for the field trip" vibes weren't doing him any favors. She'd woken up in the very late morning to his texts asking if she and Mark had talked yet in the weirdest ways possible, the last one being "Hey just checking in to see if you're getting these," followed by an unhinged amount of emojis.

There were no messages from Mark, and even though she hadn't really expected anything she'd held out hope for some kind of apology. She'd have even taken some wild rant about what a bitch she was just so she wouldn't have to be the first one to re-open the conversation.

When she'd stormed out of Mark's last night, she'd come real close to packing her bags and heading to the airport. When Henry sent the text about Mark possibly being in danger she couldn't stop thinking about it, and how the other people who lived there were in danger as well. By the next morning, she was texting Travis to ask if he could spot her the cash to buy a last-minute ticket. And the hotel, if it wasn't too much trouble. As always, she swore she'd pay him back, but also knew he'd never let her follow through on it (as if she realistically could). She hated how easy he made it, but what she hated more was the look he'd give her after she got home and asked about her trip. It'd be genuine, but with the undercurrent of "you couldn't have done it without me" he liked way too much. Especially since he knew she'd repay him in other ways, as was the theme of their situationship. She'd texted him back last night from the Uber, saying she was sorry and she missed him too.

She'd never said "I love you" before and she wasn't going to start now.

When she finally woke up she texted the Kid back that things hadn't gone well, and of course he wrote back right away, saying they were on the way to her hotel to talk. She'd barely had time to throw on leggings and a t-shirt and get a coffee from next door before they arrived. Wanting to avoid feeling like they were negotiating a seedy hotel threesome, she waited for them in the unnervingly sparse and empty lounge in the lobby.

"That's a kind way of putting it," she said.

She'd forgotten how chaotically emotional Mark was, although part of her was impressed how he made it look like he was fine and just the kind of sensitive, in touch with his feelings but kind of vulnerable guy who made you feel safe. She'd initially chalked the hook-up up to trauma wrapped in nostalgia, but in the Uber she remembered his well-practiced deep questions about her life and his unbelievably rapt attention to her answers. He'd been running a full-court press on her, and it was clearly not his first time at bat (or however sports went).

The Black Guy, clearly the teacher on this little field trip, leaned forward. Not teacher, she realized, as the lived-in looking suit, thick-rimmed glasses, close cut hair/beard combo and the patiently stern manner he had was total college professor vibes.

"Have you been able to remember anything from just being back here?" the Professor asked. "Any kind of rituals or strange language that was used? Anything that seemed out of place? Even something mundane could point to a supernatural element we're missing."

"Like I said a thousand times before, no. I was too busy being traumatized while threatened with a gun and a sword. That was out of place enough." She paused, took a drink, and added "I'm still trying to get over how fucked up it is and that this stuff is actually real."

She'd known it'd been heavily assisted by denial, but a big part of her recovery had been telling herself the whole "ghostiness" of it all was something she'd projected on to her memories. She'd gone through an embarrassing Wicca phase in college, the idea being if she knew "magic" she could keep herself safe from other "spirits." When she realized none of what she was doing was having any kind of tangible effect, she'd pivoted to a "I was wrong and confused, that stuff isn't real" stance, leading quickly to the realization of "Oh shit, I need to get into therapy."

The first call from these two had shaken the deliberate fiction that'd been keeping her from constant terror and it only seemed to be getting worse as it was confirmed things like ghosts, haunted houses, and past lives (and whatever the fuck else) were real. So real, even, there were people who dealt with it for a living.

"They are," the Professor said in a tone suggesting this wasn't the first time he'd had to ease someone into this reality. "It's just that there are too many variables at play to narrow it down, and anything could really help us out."

"Fucking crazy," she muttered. "But that sucks, and I'm sorry I don't remember anything else." It was a lie, but after how upset Mark had gotten last night she decided it was best not to volunteer anything else. "But please don't start telling me about other stuff that's real also. This took long enough to forget."

"Generally speaking, the less you know the better," the Professor said, giving her a smile. She nodded in appreciation, but then realized how intent his gaze was on her. He was sincerely concerned, she was sure it, but now she could feel his gaze on her like a physical force. This was a guy who not only deals with supernatural shit, but also PI shit and could probably spot a lie a thousand miles away. While he'd been nothing but cordial while picking her up from the airport and driving her to the hotel, she didn't want to feel that invisible pressure on her for much longer.

"Good to know," she said, standing up. "I wish I could do more, but I guess that's it."

The Kid and Henry (the gaze had shaken her into remembering) looked at each other before getting to their feet as well. Henry's right hand dropped down into his pocket and there was a clink of metal, like keys hitting loose change. The Kid glanced over at him, somehow radiating even more nervous energy. It was clear they weren't done with this, and she realized she was stuck in their orbit until her flight later that evening.

Henry sighed, taking his hand out of his pocket and extending it for a handshake. "Thank you for your time, Ms. Baker. I appreciate you coming out here for this."

"Sure thing," she said, taking his hand delicately and for just a quick shake before stepping back. "Good luck, I guess? I hope this gets taken care of and people don't get hurt."

"I hope so too," he nodded solemnly. The Kid's nerves seemed back under control now and the two of them headed for the exit. She turned back to the elevator and then she felt her phone buzz in her pocket.

It was Mark, texting to ask if they could talk.

She stopped and looked over her shoulder and saw Henry and the Kid were in deep discussion and hadn't made it to the door yet. She knew she could just get on the elevator, not write Mark back, watch a shitty movie on cable, and just get on the plane later.

Henry looked over at her, like he'd sensed her wavering. They locked eyes and he gave her that intense stare again.

"You are so fucking stupid," she said to herself. "Hey," she called, holding up her phone. "He wants to talk."

***

"Are you fucking kidding me?"

It was the welcome she'd expected from him once he realized she wasn't alone. They'd headed right over to Mark's place after she changed clothes, figuring if she was going to confront a boy about demons she should at least look cute.

"I wish," she said. "Can we just do this, please?"

With a defeated look, Mark opened the door to let them all in. "This is harassment, dude," Mark said as Henry walked by.

"Oh my god, settle down. You said you wanted to talk, and I'm going to tell them everything you'd say to me so I don't have to deal with it anymore either." She narrowed her eyes pointedly at him. "Unless you were lying and just wanted me to come over for another reason?" That reeled in his indignation.

"Look, I...," he started to tell the detectives, but he kept glancing over at her. "I'm sorry, can you give us a moment?" he said to them, nodding towards her. "If that's okay?" She gave him a nod, a little pleased with herself he was so rattled.

"Whatever you need to do," Henry said, sitting down on the sofa. The Kid was immediately enamored with what he could see of Mark's "library" and made his way over there. Mark nodded to the patio doors off the kitchen and she followed. She leaned against the railing as he closed the sliding glass door and looked back with guilt smeared all over his face.

"I'm sorry things got so...out of hand last night," he said.

"In what way? The sex or assuming I'm some kind of cheating bitch?"

"I never said you were a bitch."

"It was implied. So which is it?"

"Well, not the sex for sure," he gave her a little smile, which retreated as soon as he saw how unamused she was. "The snapping at you thing. And making assumptions about what I saw on your phone, which I probably shouldn't have looked at in the first place."

"A good start."

"Oh, come on. It's perfectly reasonable to not want to talk about horrible shit from my past with strangers."

"I'm not a stranger. I am, in fact, one of the only people still alive who also went through it. Instead of wanting to face that, you put all of your efforts into fucking me and then getting rid of me as fast as possible."

He slumped. "Okay, that's fair. But I wasn't *just* trying to fuck you. I'm sorry if I made you feel that way. I'm genuinely happy to see you and I wanted to know about your life."

"It's whatever," she said, clocking the conditionality of the 'apology.' "I'm just mad I fell for your whole...thing," she said, gesturing at him. "Just tell me, are you going to be straight with these guys or not? They clearly need a lot more than I can offer them."

"Sounded like you told them plenty," he grumbled. "What did you leave out?"

"I didn't tell them about the whole...past lives aspect and how it related to everything."

He groaned, running a hand through his hair. "Fuck, so just the worst part then."

The worst part for you, she wanted to say, but shrugged instead. "It may not even come up. It could be something else that gets them to leave us alone. I wouldn't try bullshitting them, though, because I'm pretty sure Henry will know if you're lying."

"What, through magic?" Mark said.

"Probably. Maybe. Either way he seems like the real deal"

"I was just hoping more people wouldn't find out that I'm.. .y'know?"

"I get it," she said, trying to push away how angry she was so he'd feel safe enough to open up. "But...I don't know, maybe they can fix it somehow?"

"I doubt it." He slumped against the railing, looking into the condo with a wave of anxiety cresting over his face.

"No use waiting," she said, taking him by the arm and leading him inside like the petulant child he was emulating.

"Those are some cool ass Gundams, dude," the Kid said, scurrying after them. "Do you have a favorite series, because--"

"I don't know, man," Mark said, waving him off. "I just think robots are cool."

"Right. Sorry," he said, following them back to the living room where Henry waited.

"So what do you want to know?" Mark asked as they sat down. "I think Christine, and probably the internet, told you all the high points."

"We covered a lot of ground, but I'd rather just hear it directly from you. Just start from the beginning, and try include as many details as possible," Henry said, and then added "I know a charm that can help you relax and sharpen your memory, if it helps."

"Are you for really-real with this stuff?" Mark said, squirming in his chair. "I get there's got to be something legit going on, given what we saw, but actual spells and stuff just seems..." he trailed off.

"I get that, Mr. Wa...Mark. Just an offer, although we may have to do some casting later. With your permission, of course." Henry's patient veneer seemed to crack a little, most likely from finally being this close to answers and Mark still avoiding them.

Mark shrugged, and then threw his arms up in the air with a laugh. "Shit, why not? Let's see some magic."

"It's not going to look like much," Henry said. "We're just going to be talking." His voice took on a kind of low echo, and Christine couldn't tell if it was real or imagined. "Just look at my eyes and hear the sound of my voice as you think about what happened." The echo rolled through the whole next sentence, and for a second her vision tunneled as she watched Henry's mouth move inaudibly. It took a little effort to look away, but it was clear this was all too real.

She looked at Mark instead and watched his face go slack, his mouth trying to match what Henry was whispering but failing miserably. "It's fine," Henry said, his voice thankfully returning to normal in every sense of the word. "It takes a second for it to really take hold."

Mark slumped back in his chair, rubbing his face with both hands. "Okay," he said. "That was...impressive." He put his hands down and looked around the room. "And clearly something is happening to me now, because--" the calm expression on his face skipped a beat, and then halfheartedly returned. "--yeah, I remember a lot now."

"Let's get to it, then," Henry said, laying his phone out with a recording app open as the Kid took a notebook out of his bag.

***

He told them everything, including stuff Christine had never fully known. He didn't give many specifics about the murders themselves, which was good as she wasn't sure she could take a vivid retelling of her family being attacked. When Mark was finished he let out a long exhale and wiped away the tears that started flowing almost as soon as he began. He looked over and gave her a shrug and a smile that said 'What a surprise, Mark Watson is crying again.'

"Oof," he chuckled, voice now full of the emotion he'd been suppressing. "That was not fun."

Henry looked over at the notes the Kid had taken and nodded in satisfaction. "First of all, I know talking about all that was very hard, for both of you, so thank you." He nodded at her. "Give me just a second to confer with Martin, if you don't mind."

"Confer away," Mark said in a close to normal tone of voice.

The two detectives nodded and then scurried out of the room like excited school boys. After they were out of sight, Christine leaned forward and put a hand on Mark's knee. "There's no way that kid is a colleague, right?" She whispered, hoping it'd calm him down.

Mark gave a sharp laugh as he finished wiping his eyes. "Right? He's an intern, at best." He smiled, his emotional storm letting up a bit. "I hope this didn't freak you out too much."

"Just the expected amount, but I guess it'll help in the long run. You know what they say, doing the right thing is never easy."

"I'm sure that will help me get to sleep tonight," he grumbled.

"For real," she nodded. "I feel like I haven't cared about 'the right thing' this much in my entire life."

They sat in silence for a few moments, and then Mark sat up and tried to get a look around the corner where Henry and Martin disappeared. "It does not seem great they're taking so long," he said.

"It could mean they've got answers," she said, unconvinced.

A couple of minutes later the two detectives came back into view. Their expressions were those of having answers but not really liking them.

"So," Henry said, sitting down. "What you've said, especially about the past life connection, has definitely narrowed down our options."

"I believe," Henry said, being obviously cautious in his wording, "what we're dealing with is demonic in nature."

"Fantastic," Mark said, nodding sarcastically. "It's just demonic possession. That's all, huh?"

"Not possession, per se" Henry said. "I believe what was, and still is, in the house is a demonic entity of some kind. The way Corwin was compelled to make his victims look into the flames to see something, the worshiping nature of his speech, and the ability to extend its...attentions while still being bound to a spot are part of a pretty clear pattern."

"Well I'm glad I could be so helpful," Mark said, getting to his feet. "So if we're done here...?"

Henry grimaced and waved Mark back down. "It's not that simple."

"Why would it be?" Mark rolled his eyes and dropped back onto the couch.

"There's not a lot of consensus about past lives in my line of work," Henry said. "They can be remembered, and at times affect the current one when there's unfinished business or a supernatural encounter. Clearly Corwin had one, and that's how you've ended up with this connection."

"Connection is a way to put it," Mark said, looking away.

"I know, but I'll just say you two are different people by every possible measurement and leave it at that. It does, however, leave us with a fairly significant problem. In some ways, demons are like radiation. They leave traces wherever they go, and it can have lasting effects. Everything Corwin did, and especially the sacrifices he did in its name, exposed him quite a bit. And that's without knowing how long this entity had been affecting him before the killings started."

"So I have cancer," Mark said. "Demon cancer, no less."

"In a sense," Henry said. "When I put the charm on you I could sense demonic energy still with you." Out of the corner of her eye, Christine saw Martin look in confusion instead of just nodding intently as he had been. "It's how it was able to control you. And, if it gets more of its strength back, be able to do it again."

Mark shot out of his chair. "No. No fucking way. Cut it out, whatever it takes. I'm not going through that again." He paced through the room in sudden and total mania. "Get rid of it, and if you can't I'll throw myself in front of a train or something."

"Whoa," Martin said. "Suicide's never the answer."

"Shut up, intern!" Mark snarled, lunging at him. "You may've heard all my disgusting shit but you have no *idea* what it was like!" Martin leapt back, almost losing his balance.

Mark turned and started to pace frantically, rubbing his hands together like he was trying to get them clean. "It used me to kill all those people, and made sure I remembered all of it! I'm not going to let it take me again. No way. I'd rather die than be a killer for it again."

"It's okay," Henry said, moving between Mark and the rest of them with his arms wide to signal he wasn't a threat. "We can fix this."

Mark turned away, fingers clawing through his hair. "Shit. Shit, shit, shit. It's going to be bad, isn't it?" He looked back at Henry, his voice now soft and childlike. "I'm going to have to go back there, aren't I?"

Henry nodded in confirmation and apology. "I'm afraid so."

Mark dropped to his knees and screamed at the top of his lungs, sending Christine out of her seat and back a few steps before she realized she'd moved. The scream petered out into a low howl, and Mark rubbed his face with both palms, smearing fresh tears and snot away.

"Okay," he said, getting to his feet. "Let's get this thing out of me."

Chapter Six

Henry explained it wasn't that simple, but assured them this was one of their specialties, leaving out his own equally horrific entanglements with demonic forces.

"Some demons," he explained once everyone had re-settled, "grow in power through various forms of worship, and human sacrifice is an incredibly potent one. Corwin's acts and eventual conversion of the other boy, Darren, gave it massive amounts of power. Darren's suicide in the house later was an even more powerful sacrifice, and it was probably commanded by the demon so it could sustain itself over the years. It also gave Darren the ability to take control of you."

"Because Corwin's soul, my soul, was full of demon cancer," Mark said matter-of-factly. His outbursts had worn him out, and now he held his head in his hands and stared off into space.

"Exactly," Henry said, not wanting to quibble with the terminology.

"Not all the murders happened in the house," Christine said. She'd gone and refilled her Starbucks cup with wine during their break, and when she returned she sat on the couch as far away from Mark as possible. "What about their souls or whatever? Are they..."

"They aren't tied to the demon, no," Henry said, sparing her from directly asking about her brother. "The people killed outside of the house were done in its name, though. Still a sacrifice, but not as potent. More than likely just enough to wake it up and let it start building up power again."

"And it made me bring all of them," Mark waved weakly toward Christine, "to the house. So it could get itself a real meal."

Henry nodded. "That's what it still wants. If it gets powerful enough, it'll be able to use the sacrificed souls to do its bidding."

"Jesus," Christine said, and she and Mark looked at each other for the first time since his outburst. "That's how many?"

"Six," Mark said without a pause.

"Eventually," Henry continued, "it'll be strong enough to send them off the property to start gathering more, not to mention affect Mark again."

"And that'll happen when, precisely?"

"I don't know, so it's best to get started right away. Everything being concentrated at spot does make things easier, as I can banish it and break those spirits free all at once."

"And I'd have to be there too, of course," Mark said.

"We could try banishing it here, but there's no guarantee it'll be drawn back to the house. It could just as easily find a way to attach itself to something, or someone, else. It's your call, though."

Mark shook his head. "I'm not taking any chances. I can't go through this again."

"Okay then." Henry ran a hand over his beard before he moved on to the other bad news. "Before we do that, we need to figure out where this presence came from. It'd have to be some kind of prolonged contact or major incident."

"It's not just an evil house or whatever?" Christine asked.

"If that were the case, this would have been over when the house burned down. That's what's been throwing me." He didn't like to project anything but confidence in front of a client, but he knew how much he'd need to impress the importance of the next step so Mark didn't freak out again.

"I don't remember anything else," Mark said with exasperation. "Just what Darren showed me and the flashes of Corwin's life at the end."

"I figured as much. You weren't going to be shown anything you could use against it. To find out I'll have to go deeper into your mind this time, all the way back into Corwin's memories."

"Oh," Martin piped up. "I've done that before. It's...fun. Well, fine. You'll be fine." Henry looked over his shoulder pointedly at him and he quickly went back to typing.

"Don't oversell it," Mark grumbled.

"There's no danger," Henry said, forcing a smile. "I've done it numerous times and Martin's was a unique circumstance. In fact, we have everything we need for it in the car." He stood up. "If you'll excuse me. Martin?" He looked up. "Can you give me a hand?" Henry said through clenched teeth.

"Uh, sure." Martin said in obvious discomfort as he got to his feet.

"I'm going to need more wine," Christine said, heading into the kitchen as Henry and Martin went to the car.

Halfway there, Henry stopped Martin with a hand on his arm. "We need to work on your people skills," he said, which was the kindest way he could think to put it.

Martin winced. "That bad, huh? I'm sorry, you know I babble when I get nervous."

"You need to be less nervous, then. If you can't project confidence to the client then they can get skittish. And Mark's as skittish as it gets." Henry kept walking, hoping his tone wasn't too harsh.

"For sure, for sure," Martin said, trailing after him. When he caught up with Henry at the trunk of the Gremlin, he continued. "So I was wondering...you said you could sense the presence in

Mark from doing the charm, but I thought you could only do something like that with a more intense connection, so--"

"Look," Henry said, pulling out one of the several bags tucked into the hidden compartment in the trunk and thrusting it at him. "I may have taught you everything you know about magic, but I haven't taught you everything *I* know, got it?"

Martin audibly gulped. "Oh. Okay. I'm so--"

"Save it," Henry said, the irritation he had with him since his conversation with John boiling over. "And while we're at it, do *not* talk to my kids about magic again. They are to be as far away from this as possible. Clear?" He walked back towards the condo without waiting for a response. After a long pause he heard Martin hurry to catch up.

"Yes, sir," he said in a quavering voice making Henry feel like he'd stepped on a puppy's tail. "I'm sorry. Really. It won't happen again."

"I know," Henry said, guilt now far outweighing the thrill of laying into someone you thought deserved it. "Just be better, okay?"

"For sure," Martin said, relief creeping into his voice. "Will do."

When they came back inside he saw Christine had filled her cup to nearly overflowing and Mark was rolling himself a joint. He looked up at Henry just as he was about to lick it shut and said, "Is this okay?"

"I mean, I'd prefer my family not smell it on me when I get home," Henry said, taking off his jacket and laying it on the back of a chair. "My kids would never let me hear the end of it."

"For later, then." Mark licked and sealed the joint before putting it back in the humidor.

Henry rolled up his sleeves and motioned towards the table in the kitchen. "We need to set up a circle, just to make sure nothing gets loose."

"I'm so glad that's a possibility," Mark said, walking into the kitchen and pulling out a chair. He nodded at Christine and said in a low voice. "Does she need to be here? Especially if there's a chance something could happen."

"They're my ride," Christine called from the living room. "And I'd kind of feel like shit Ubering back to my hotel after talking you into this."

"Fair enough," Mark said, and he and Martin began moving furniture out of the way while Henry sifted through the vials in his bag for the one with the most potency. Once they got Mark into the center seat, Henry took out the large wet-erase marker and began to plot out the circle while adding various glyphs and warding symbols. "Don't worry," he said, catching Mark's concerned look. "A little Windex and it comes right off." He started writing and then added, "You do have a vacuum, right? That'll help with the salt-mixture cleanup."

"Despite appearances, yes," Mark said, agitation growing. Henry considered letting him smoke up anyway, but figured it'd be best not to chance anything. Once the circle was prepared, Henry got to his feet with a groan and a flare of pain from his bum knee. Martin signaled from outside the circle he was ready, and Henry moved behind Mark's chair and laid his hands gently on his shoulders.

"If all goes well," Henry said, patting Mark on the shoulder, "you'll feel like you woke up from a dream."

"Did you hear the part where I dreamed about my body being used for murder?" Mark said, taking a deep breath. "Am I supposed to relax or something?"

"That'd help," Henry said, closing his eyes and reciting the spell to himself from memory.

"Well, I don't think there's much of a c--"

"--ome on, Corwin! Keep up, or I'm going to think you don't care about getting your pecker wet," DiBenzo called back to him over the chaos in the street. Justin pushed his way through them, still not used to the crowded and hectic Calcutta streets, even after six months of being stationed here.

They'd been told helping the British keep their hold on India and keeping the Japs from getting further into China was vital, especially since the fall of Burma, but they hadn't seen any action at all. Not that he was eager to, but he'd expected he'd be "doing his part" on the front lines, not helping the Brits keep their hold over a people who clearly didn't want them there. He thought the occasional trip into Manhattan with his folks when he was a kid would have prepared him for anything, but this was like nothing he'd ever imagined. Children and adults lined the streets begging for food, while the flow of factory workers employed by the Brits (mostly Burmese refugees) both ignored and surrounded them.

He'd started hanging out with DiBenzo because he was the only one in the unit also from Jersey, but that was where their similarities ended. DiBenzo was allegedly a Catholic, but the way he drank and whored around made Justin think he had a different definition than his. Burly and loud, DiBenzo seemed to enjoy Justin's nervous and proper demeanor, dragging him to bars, brothels, and other raucous joints on nearly every one of their weekend passes. This time was no different, and now he was dragging him deeper into the city, claiming he knew of the perfect "professional" who could help Justin with what DiBenzo called "a terminal case of virgin-itis." Justin had known confiding in him had been a bad idea, but he couldn't hold his liquor as well as Benzo could. This often led to tearful confessions of fears and insecurities being used to "playfully" tease Justin later.

"I'm coming, I'm coming," he said, mumbling an apology to the women in Benzo's wake he'd roughly shoved past.

"You will be, Corwin," Benzo said, reaching back and pulling him up along side him with a thick arm. "These Indian chicks are expertly trained, y'see? They got this thing, a karma-suit-a-ra, and they get all bendy and flexible. I was able to bend this one around like a damn pretzel last time. I'll show you how its done."

"Great," Justin said, terror creeping up his spine. It was bad enough he was being dragged to what was probably a disgusting brothel, but apparently Benzo was going to be supervising the whole affair. Here he was thinking his first time was going to be on his wedding night, not being watched over by the guy who regularly farted into his pillow.

Benzo yanked him off to the side and into an alley that seemed to appear out of nowhere. They stumbled down it for a few paces, and then Benzo stopped to look around as he emptied the bottle he'd been carrying in his other hand.

"Are we lost?" Justin asked, praying in his head as hard as he could. "Because I'm sure we'll get another pass some time, and they're playing--"

"Nah, shut up," Benzo said, tossing the bottle away. "I just needed to get my bearings." He lurched forward again, dragging Justin through a maze of narrow alleys where suspicious and frightened eyes watched them from behind curtains and corners.

"I don't think we're supposed to be here," Justin said, discomfort multiplying. "The guidebook said we should avoid--"

"Screw the guidebook," Benzo said, coming to a stop and looking back and forth between two doors on opposite sides of the alley. "Here we go," he said, deciding on one and proceeding to pound on it with his fist.

"This, ah, doesn't look like a...well, you know."

"Because it ain't a 'y'know,'" Benzo winked. "I never said she was a professional. Just a really talented amateur. I followed her home after I scooped her up last time because I knew I'd want seconds." Somehow, Justin realized, this had gotten worse. Before he could say anything, the door opened a crack and the sliver of a face peered at them. The eye went wide with surprise upon seeing Benzo, who just grinned and shouldered his way into the house. The middle aged Indian man who had opened the door tumbled to the ground, and there was a shriek from further in the apartment sounding like a young woman's.

"Benzo!" Justin called after him as the bigger man staggered down the hallway towards it. Justin knelt down to try to help the man up, but he was screaming at him in whatever language they spoke and flailing his arms trying to get Justin away. "I'm sorry!" he said, hoping the clasped hands and bowing conveyed the right message. Did they even bow here? He asked himself as he hurried in the direction DiBenzo had lumbered.

The place was nicer than Justin would have imagined from the outside, and larger too. He ducked his head into the rooms off the hallway until he came to the end and rounded the corner. The room looked like a mixture of a bedroom and living room, with banners and other decorations on the walls. Benzo stood in the middle, hand gripping the upper arm of a girl who couldn't be older than twenty.

She yelled again, pelting Benzo with kicks and punches he was laughing off.

"She's a real spitfire," Benzo said, a feral glaze filling his eyes. "Let me loosen her up for you and then you can have your turn."

"No," Justin said, waving his hands so emphatically he surprised himself. "Let's just go, okay? Let's g--"

"Go!" the man, the girl's father or guardian or whatever, yelled in heavily accented English as he pushed past Justin. "You go now! Get out!" It wasn't the smaller man's yells drawing Benzo's focus but the large butcher knife he'd picked up on his way.

"Look," Benzo said, letting her go and turning his attention to the older man. "Just shut up and--"

The man slashed at Benzo's out stretched hand. Benzo tried to grab it but the knife cut deep into the side of his palm.

"Motherfucker!" Benzo snapped, jerking his hand back and flinging droplets of blood across the room. The man advanced but Benzo, who loved to "mix it up," slid forward and landed a crushing jab into the smaller man's face. He gave a surprised gurgle, barely audible over the girl's screaming. "You fucking cut me," Benzo said, smacking the knife out of the man's loose grip before grabbing the front of his shirt and decking him again.

Justin saw the girl start to lunge forward but he beat her to it, shoving Benzo from behind with the effect of a gnat trying to move a rhino. "DiBenzo!" Justin yelled, in as close a tone to their Sergeant as he could muster. "Let's go!"

Without even looking, Benzo shoved Justin back, sending him stumbling into the far wall. Justin lost his footing in a tangle of rugs and fell on his ass. The impact on the wall shook the trinkets and shelves on it, and then the contents of one fell on his head. Tiny statues and other knickknacks pelted him, and then a long, thin object bounced off his skull and landed in his lap. It was a cane, Justin realized, wrapped in beads and other decorative papers like it was a museum piece of some sort.

Justin went to toss it aside, but as soon as he wrapped his hand around it he felt a jolt like he'd put his hand on a hot stove. It clattered to the ground next to him, and Justin realized despite the chaos and screaming he couldn't keep his eyes off it.

He picked it up, ready to toss it away if it was somehow still hot, but it had subsided to a dull heat spreading up Justin's arm and settling right behind his eyes. He stood up, hand gripping the cane tighter, and the silver top of the cane, an elegant, curving sculpture of fire, caught the light and flashed into his eye. Benzo shoved the girl to the ground and then slammed the man into the wall again, even though he already looked like he was unconscious.

Justin shoved Benzo again, the cane still in his hand. He should probably drop it but he didn't really want to.

"What the hell are you doing, Corwin? I'm trying to help you out here," Benzo said, poking Justin in the chest so hard it pushed him back against the wall again.

"Let's just go," Justin said, a panicked whine creeping into his voice.

"You take your little souvenir and go. I'm not done yet," Benzo grinned like an animal, turning back to the bleeding and unconscious man. The girl cowered in the corner, her path to the only door blocked by the crowd of men. She'd stopped screaming and now was looking at Justin in abject terror, as if this was his fault. His hand squeezed the cane hard, the heat from it rising again.

"Hey!" Justin snapped, his voice louder. "I said let's go!"

Benzo turned back to him again, all traces of amusement gone. "The fuck you say?"

As Benzo took a step forward, Justin adjusted his grip on the cane. His thumb had moved up against the base of the silver top and he could feel a little button there. Not thinking about it, Justin flicked it and then reached over with his other hand, grabbed the top, and pulled it free from the cane. There was another gleaming flash of light, and then Justin swung the piece of metal from the inside of the cane upward with a nervous yell.

Benzo stopped.

They both looked down as the bottom half of Benzo's tie fell to the ground. Before it touched the floor a gush of red sprung forth from the line across his lower chest.

"What?" Benzo said, dropping down on one knee, hands moving to keep as much of the viscera starting to ooze out of him in place. Justin backed up, hitting the wall. He scooted sideways along the

wall, his feet trying to move him further from the blood gushing from DiBenzo's chest and stomach. The girl started shrieking again, and the man began to stir. When he raised his head and opened his eyes as much as the swelling would allow he let out a scream of his own.

"Shut up!" Justin yelled, and as he did Benzo began to let out a slow, worried moan.

"I said shut up!" Justin screamed again. He swung the thing in his right hand again and it slashed across Benzo's face, taking his nose and several teeth off this time.

A sword, Justin realized. It's a sword hidden in a cane.

Benzo's moan had turned into wet flapping as his jaw opened wider than it should, now held in place by just the meat of one of his cheeks. His tongue lolled out aimlessly and then he fell forward. The girl was still wailing and the man stood up, holding out his hands to Justin as he got up on his knees. "No!" he shouted. "You give! Bad thing, very bad!"

Justin clenched the sheath and the hilt of the blade tighter as it felt like a blaze was erupting from inside them. No, Justin thought, Not give.

Mine.

He backed toward the door and the man crawled towards him, hands still reaching out for it. Justin swung the sheath at him, smacking away his greedy, grabbing little hands.

"No!" Justin roared again, stumbling into the hallway. He turned and ran toward the door, absentmindedly flicking what blood he could off the blade before sliding it home without even having to think about it.

He barreled out into the alley, weakly trying to pull the door shut behind him. When that failed he took off running and turned the first corner he came to. He slowed, trying to look nonchalant as he walked with the cane. The bottom of it tapped against the street, and Justin felt himself leaning into it like it had always been a part of him.

***

"Fuck you," Mark called from the bathroom in between bouts of vomiting and dry heaving. "Waking up from a dream my ass, dude!" He retched again and Henry headed back into the kitchen, where Christine was leaning against the wall and twirling hair around her fingers at an alarming pace.

"I feel like my confidence in your abilities goes down a little every time we see each other," she said, turning her attention to him.

"I'm sorry," he said, trying to keep his tone neutral. "This keeps becoming more and more complex, but I'm confident we know everything we need to."

"See, I just didn't think it'd take this long for us to get there though," she said, walking towards the kitchen. She stopped right before crossing the barrier of the circle still drawn on the tile. She sighed and turned around. "I don't need another drink that badly," she said.

"No shit," Mark said, coming out of the bathroom and wiping his mouth and chin with a towel. "Let me guess: my demon cancer is terminal."

"We can still exorcise this from you," Henry said, remembering to use his calming tones. "All this means is we're dealing with a presence a little more powerful than I thought. It's challenging, but not insurmountable."

"I do so love a challenge," Mark snapped, walking past Henry and into the living room. "I'm absolutely smoking that joint now, by the way."

"That's fair," Henry nodded.

Martin came back inside the condo and headed for the sink. "For the record," he said to Mark, "your dumpster is very hard to find." Mark had yelled for them to "get that shit out of here" while he was running to the bathroom after waking up. Once they'd quickly swept up the salt mixture from the edges of the circle, Martin had volunteered to take it outside.

"Sorry it was so *challenging*," Mark said, passing the joint to Christine next to him.

Martin looked about to snap back but Henry waved him off. "It's alright. You've got to remember most people aren't used to this," Henry said, bringing Martin back into the kitchen with him and talking low enough so Mark and Christine couldn't hear. "Even if they've had an encounter."

Before Martin could respond, Mark hollered "You're scrubbing that off my floor, right?"

Martin nodded to Henry in annoyed understanding.

"Now," Henry said. "I've been down on my hands and knees enough today, so I'll spray while you wipe. Deal?"

With many hands making less work, the two of them had all traces of the supernatural off the floor by the time Mark and Christine had stopped smoking. "Are we good to talk?" Henry asked, walking into the now-hazy room.

"I thought you didn't want your clothes to get smelly," Mark said. The anger had left his voice, but there was still an edge to it.

"I'll manage," Henry said, a little grateful for the second-hand smoke so his own irritation wouldn't start showing.

"So what's the prognosis, doc?" Mark said when Henry sat down.

"Like I said, we're still on track, and I'm sorry the memory was so jarring. It takes a very strong presence to project like that, even with you still being connected to it." Henry said. "So this demon was bound to the blade at some point, and powerful enough it could latch on to Justin that fast. You said shortly after he got home he killed his parents, and disposing of their bodies in the furnace freed it from the blade and let it take up residence there. Despite the fuel from the murders ten years ago, it still didn't have the strength to escape when the house was destroyed. That means not only did it take residency in the ground, but it's more powerful than your average demon."

Mark smiled "I've always been a fan of being above average. So what does that mean for us now?"

"It means I'm going to have to head back to the office and get some more powerful gear. Do you know where the cane ended up after everything?"

Mark shrugged. "Last I saw it I was using it to lock my high school bully's demon-possessed corpse in a murder furnace. Which is not a sentence I ever expected to say."

"It's a sentence no one should say," Christine added. "Half those things shouldn't even exist."

"And yet here we are," Mark said, throwing his hands up in amused exasperation.

"Okay," Henry said, trying to regain their attention. "With the house burned down around it--"

"Plus it exploded," Christine interjected.

"The furnace, not the house," Mark added.

"Guys," Henry said, having to dip into his angry Dad tone.

"Okay, okay," Mark said. "So when are we doing this?"

"As soon as possible, so once we get back from the city with supplies. Are you good with that?"

"I absolutely am not," Mark said. "But at the same time, knowing the full extent of this fucked-up-edness, plus the fact I might be used as a murder-puppet again, is quite motivating. So tonight it is."

"Good," Henry nodded, getting to his feet. "Ms. Baker, we can drop you by your hotel on the way?"

"He's so formal," Christine said to Mark.

"It's what you like to see in a magic, demon-hunting exorcist," he replied with a solemn nod.

"Christine," Henry said with a pointed look.

"Right," she said, looking over at Mark. "I'm gonna hang out for a bit, if that's okay?"

"Hundred percent," Mark nodded.

"I'll text you when we're on our way back," Henry said, picking up his bag and heading for the door with Martin close at his heels. He was more than happy to leave those two do what was needed to process everything that'd been dumped in their laps.

Trauma bonds were a hell of a thing after all.

Chapter Seven

"So who is he?" Mark asked after they'd finished. "Travis, I mean."

It was hard to remember who initiated, but he was sure they'd started making out before Professor and the Kid (as Christine called them) had left the parking lot. He stopped before their clothes came off to ask if she was still mad at him, and she rolled her eyes and told him to shut up. This time they hadn't made it to the bedroom, just stayed on the couch and fucked so intensely Mark forgot the impending horror looming over him for a while.

"He's just a guy," Christine said. She was laying her head on Mark's chest, and he had his arm around her to keep her from rolling off the inconveniently narrow couch.

Mark made skeptical noise.

"What does that mean?" she asked.

"I mean, if he's not family or a close friend, then why is he saying 'I love you?' Just a little curious, that's all." He was more than just curious but he hoped it didn't show.

She glared at him, and Mark was worried he'd kicked off another fight.

The annoyed look faded and she shrugged. "He's just a guy. He's very interested in me and I'm..."

"Not?" Mark added after the pause.

"Cautious. He's a nice guy, nothing really wrong with him, but it's just...whatever. We spend time together, go places and stuff. It's nice, I guess."

"And do you, y'know?" He raised his eyebrows in a not so subtle manner.

She paused for long enough a 'No' would be unbelievable.

"Sometimes. Not often. But don't worry, you're *much* better than he is." She said in a deeply condescending tone, as she patted him on the chest.

He narrowed his eyes. "That's not what this is about. I just don't want to get in the middle of something. I've done that plenty." He'd lost track of the number of times he was told by women he was looking to "reconnect" with that they had new boyfriends who didn't want her to talk to him.

"I bet."

There was a pause and then he said, "I'm going to go out on a limb here, and stop me if I'm wrong, but would there be an age-gap element to this non-romance romance you have?"

"Not really," she said, blushing and somehow making her look even prettier.

"Not a no. What are we talking, twenty years? Fifteen?"

"No!" she snapped, and then mumbled something indistinct.

"What was that?" He held his free hand up to his ear.

She glared at him and said. "Ten years is not a big deal."

"Ha!" he barked, raising his hand and pointing his forefinger in the air.

"Like you haven't chased younger women before," she said, sitting up.

"That's fair," he said, again worried he'd fucked things up again. "But," he couldn't resist adding, "Ten years younger would be a crime. But I'm just teasing. We both have our issues, no judgment."

"Good," she said. She bent down to pick up her bra and then thought better of it. "Y'know what? I'm going to take a shower, sober up a little bit, and then you can take me back to my hotel."

"I said I was sorry," he said.

Way to fuck things up again, Romeo.

"I'm not mad," she said, shimmying the rest of the way out of her skirt. "I just need to pack, change clothes, and check out. Then we can head over to Briarcliff."

"What do you mean 'we?'" he asked as he followed her to the bathroom.

"My flight doesn't leave until this evening. I'm not going to just sit around in the airport waiting for some text saying 'Devil killed, thumbs-up emoji'."

"He said it's going to be dangerous." Mark grabbed her arm lightly and turned her to face him. "You don't have to do this."

She took his face in her hands and looked at him intently. "I don't *have* to do anything, but I have the incredibly stupid urge to make sure this thing is actually finished. I don't want another text in ten years about all this. Besides, this thing killed my brother and crippled my Dad, so I'd really like to see it get destroyed." She pulled his head down and gave him a quick kiss. "I'll leave some hot water for you."

"We coul--" he started, but her head immediately shook.

"No, the logistics never work. Plus, it's my last chance to talk myself out of this." She let him go and then closed the bathroom door in his face.

"This could be my last night on Earth," he called out. "*Our* last night on Earth, even."

"I'll take my chances," she yelled back as the shower started running.

***

After she packed, changed, and checked out they had time for a late lunch at one of the chain places always lurking around hotels, malls, and airports. She'd been quiet the whole time, and their eatin' good was fraught with uncomfortable silences in the neighborhood.

"Are we okay?" he said when they got back in the Jeep. "I hope you're not regretting...y'know."

She looked at him askance and then smiled. "Yeah, it's fine. And I'm not having regrets or anything." She paused, and then said. "That's a lie. I have lots of regrets, but they're mostly about how I act when things get crazy. Sex isn't really the cure-all you think it's going to be in the moment."

"Ah," he said, starting the car. "I just hope I didn't make it worse."

No more than you already have, you mean.

"You didn't, so don't worry about it, okay?" She smiled at him and he smiled back, knowing he'd absolutely worry about it.

The rest of the drive was quiet, and when they crossed into Cedar Ridge he gripped the steering wheel tighter, not realizing he was doing it until she asked if he was okay.

"Not even a little bit," he said. "I haven't been back here since I collected my stuff from my Uncle's house." She gave him a comforting pat on the thigh and he almost told her how much it meant she was still here. Her phone buzzed before he could embarrass himself, and it was Henry and Martin letting them know they were on their way back. Plenty of time, he realized, to sit in a parked car and continue to be overwhelmed by memories of the time they'd been together.

When they reached Briarcliff he parked at the first available spot he saw, about a block and a half from the source of his life's misery. It was early in the evening, the summer sun already behind the hill where the affluent Cedar Ridge residents lived in the gigantic houses he always both hated and coveted. They sat in silence, Christine scrolling through her phone and Mark trying to replace thoughts of how horrible this was going to be with the pleasant memories he had of Christine. There weren't a lot, honestly, but enough to make him question if it'd been the best relationship he'd ever been in (once you removed the fear and murder from the equation).

"Can I ask you something?" he said, unable to restrain his curiosity.

Now it was her turn to give him the side-eye. "I guess?"

"It's nothing bad, I just...I was just wondering what you saw in me. In high school, I mean. I was such a mess, but you really made me feel special. And that's why I got so...well, you know."

"I don't know," she said. "It was just..."

She trailed off and the pause was interminable.

"Forget it." he said, forcing a smile. "That spell or whatever just has me in my feelings." He wasn't lying, but the fact they were just hanging and he wasn't trying to impress and then fuck her put him in unfamiliar territory.

"You just took me off guard, relax," she said. "I just...I needed a friend. And you were nice. And it probably didn't hurt I could tell you thought I was pretty."

"That obvious, huh?" he laughed, somehow feeling even more foolish. "Well, I'm glad I could help you out."

"Mark," she said, putting a hand on his arm. "I was getting used to another new school in another new state, and that's just how I survived. I drifted until someone noticed and picked me up."

He nodded, hoping he looked dispassionate about it. "Makes sense. I just feel bad you had such shitty luck in who did the picking."

"It's not like you knew all *this*," she waved up the street, "was going to happen. I don't blame you. Anymore." The last bit was quiet, but it was confirmation of what he'd worried about for years, and the reason why he never reached out to her.

"That makes one of us," he said, looking back out the window. He'd spent his whole childhood wondering what he'd done wrong to deserve having his parents and then his Aunt die, leaving him with an Uncle who didn't want him and the overwhelming urge to panic if someone looked at him the wrong way. When he found out about his past life and what he (no, *Justin*) had done it made everything make sense. Therapists had told him things don't happen to people because they deserve it, but he wondered what they'd think if he'd shared his memories of child murder and dismemberment.

After a couple years, when things began to turn around for him, he started to think being made to kill the people who cared the most about him had balanced the scales, but now he realized he should have known better. Those were just more deaths he was responsible for, and he hadn't paid the real price for them yet.

Looks like you're going to pay now, huh? For Clara, and Steve, and Christine's brother, and Ms. Kennedy. Even Uncle Joe, although that one hasn't really keep you up at night.

He shook his head, trying to shut off that side of him again. If the kids in school had known how much his own brain bullied him they'd have saved themselves the trouble.

"So what about Steve?" he said, grasping for the last big question that'd loomed over him for years.

"Ah," she said. "Yeah, unfortunately that was also part of the pattern. Shoring up my self worth by making sure I was noticed and pursued, which was pretty fucked up. But it seemed easier than letting people get to know me, especially since there was a chance we could move away at a moment's notice."

"I get that," he said, not getting it at all, but realizing bringing up his dead best friend she'd made out with was not as distracting as he'd thought. Especially given how Mark had murdered him just up the street. "Fucking high school, right?"

"The worst," she said with a weak smile.

He stopped asking questions, and eventually she went back to looking at her phone. Mark stared out the window, trying not to think about anything and failing miserably.

***

By the time Henry and Martin arrived the last bits of sunlight had just disappeared. They parked their faded yellow Gremlin across the street, and even from a distance made Mark wonder how it could still be running.

"Are you ready for this?" Mark asked before they got out.

"I don't think that's possible," she said.

"Fair enough."

They walked over to the car, where Martin and Henry were rooting around in the trunk. Henry had changed into a light jacket, dark turtleneck, and jeans and Martin was dressed in the junior version. Mark wasn't sure what he expected for their "work clothes," but a pointy hat and robes hadn't been out of the question. Henry took a well-worn leather satchel from the trunk, and when he turned around and saw Christine his calm demeanor seemed to crack for a moment.

"You don't have to be here, Christine," he said. "There's a good chance it's going to be dangerous."

Mark shrugged. "I tried to tell her."

"I'm a big girl," Christine said, an edge in her voice. "I'm not going to just sit around in the airport and wait for this to be over."

Henry obviously wasn't pleased but still nodded in acquiescence. "Fair enough, but you don't have to come inside"

She smiled at him. "I came all this way, so why not? Even if it's completely insane."

"Anyway," Mark said. "What's the plan?"

"I've been texting Tim," Martin said, gesturing up the street, "but he stopped responding the other day. I let him know earlier I was stopping by with friends to take a look at what's wrong with his basement, so theoretically he knows we're coming. I was hoping he'd gone out of town or something but his car is in the driveway."

"We're going to walk up nice and normal," Henry said, "and then get him to leave before we go to work."

"Just casually kick him out of his house?" Christine asked.

"I can be very persuasive," Henry said. Both seemed to be appropriate. "Once he's gone, we head to the basement and I drive the presence out of Mark. If the demon doesn't react to us, that'll definitely wake it up. At that point, Martin is going to cover you while you both get out, and once you're all clear I'll banish the demon."

"I'm guessing it's going to be more difficult than it sounds," Mark said.

"Most likely," Henry said. "But not something I haven't handled before."

"No offense," Christine said, nodding at Martin, "but you're sure he'll be able to keep us from getting murdered or possessed or whatever?"

"Martin's been studying with me for a few years and he's been an excellent student. Plus, he was able to push back the specters it generated before, so I'm confident he'll be able to keep you safe."

Christine looked over at Mark and smiled. "I told you he was an intern."

Mark couldn't help but chuckle at the hurt expression on Martin's face. "I'm not an intern. I'm an apprentice, and I get paid."

"They pay interns sometimes," Christine said.

"Okay, true but...," Martin looked over at Henry for help.

"He's not an intern," Henry said, giving Martin a reassuring pat on the shoulder. "He has plenty of experience with this, and I trust him with my life. You should too." That chased the hurt expression off Martin's face, and he actually blushed in an "Aw shucks" kind of way.

"In terms of possession," Henry continued, reaching into the satchel. "I've got these." He handed Mark a pair of beaded bracelets with gold and silver charms dangling from them. "They'll keep the demon from accessing your mind. You may still feel it trying, but it won't be able to control you."

"You're sure about that?" Mark asked, looking at them skeptically. "This isn't some 'the power was in you all along' shit?"

"I've used them plenty of times," Henry said. "On myself as well. This thing may be old and powerful but it still has weaknesses."

"You're the expert," Mark said, looping them tightly around each wrist, making sure they couldn't slip off.

"Alright," Henry said. "Let's get to work."

***

When the house came into view Mark chuckled at what had become of the infamous Cedar Ridge Murder House which had caused him misery across two lifetimes. The original had been set far back from the street, obscured by jungle-esque lawn and unkempt hedges so tall you could only catch a glimpse of the dark and crumbling roof from the sidewalk. If you pushed your way through the bushes where there'd once been an opening to the stone path, the smaller than expected house waited, sagging in on itself like it was drawing back to pounce. It was mostly wood, with some simple brick columns supporting the overhang on the treacherously decaying porch. Whatever color it had been faded to diseased gray, and the front door had turned an ominous black.

This house, however, was built to show itself off. It was closer to the sidewalk, with a perfectly maintained lawn and vibrant flower beds nestled against the house. Tiny lights illuminated the path to the front door, which was a bright red and lit in a soft and inviting manner. The house was taller than the previous structure and wide enough to be obnoxiously close to its neighbor on one side, with a long driveway on the other where a black Porsche was parked. The place was somehow both boxy and angular, with plenty of windows placed around the front seemingly at random, and even a small row at the bottom hinting there was a cozy basement underneath which absolutely had not been used for murder.

"Well that's a glow-up," Christine said as they walked up the path. Even so, it still made Mark uneasy. He couldn't tell if it was because of the obnoxious modern excess of it or because he knew there was a demon lurking underneath.

The lights inside were on but they couldn't see anyone. Once at the door, Henry waved Mark and Christine to the side of the doorbell camera while Martin rang it. They waited a couple of seconds and then he rang again. This time they could hear running footsteps from the other side, and then the door opened enough for a guy Martin's age to peer out.

"What the hell, bro?" he asked. As he looked past Martin to the rest of them his expression hardened.

"Tim, hey buddy," Martin said with a wide, fake smile. "I texted but you must not have gotten it. I remembered what you said about the problems you were having with your basement, so I brought my plumber friends over to take a look. This is the one night they're free before they head back home so I figured I'd bring them over real quick."

Tim looked at them in confusion, opening the door a little wider. "Thanks, I guess? But it's not a good time. I'm, y'know, entertaining and it's not like there's an emergency."

"You'd be surprised," Henry said. "These kinds of things get worse the longer you put them off and can really affect the property value."

"I'm willing to risk it," Tim said, closing the door. Mark stepped forward, stopping it with his foot.

Tim looked down at it and then up at Mark with what he assumed was the smaller man's "tough guy" face. "My guy," Tim said, "this is not okay."

"Neither is a plumbing emergency," Mark said, putting his hand on the door and pushing it open. Tim tried to resist it, but Mark outweighed him by about twenty-five pounds, most of it being muscle.

"Dude, what the fuck? Get out of here," Tim snapped as the rest of the group followed Mark inside. He took up position threateningly close to Tim, arms crossed and feet planted. It'd been a while since he'd had to fight someone (thanks foster system), but this guy was definitely making Mark want to give it a go.

"The thing is," Martin continued with an "aw shucks what can you do" smile and shrug, "the work is going to be really noisy and smelly and unpleasant, so maybe you guys should just head out for a little bit, huh? Hit a bar, catch a movie, y'know?"

Tim looked from Mark to Martin in irritation, and then noticed Henry and Christine making their way further into the expansive front room, complete impressive stone fireplace, that dominated most of the first floor. He was about to say something when a younger woman who may or may not have been out of high school emerged from the archway at the opposite side of the room.

"Tim? Is everything okay?" she said, confused in a way which could very well have been her natural state.

"Absolutely not," Christine said, walking over to her. "I cannot believe Tim would do this to me, especially with our baby on the way."

"Bitch, what the fuck!" Tim said, turning to follow her.

Mark reached out and placed a firm hand on Tim's chest before he could get very far. "Yeah, we're not doing that," he said, moving in front of him.

"Look buddy--" Tim started, but Mark cut him off.

"I'm not your buddy, guy. And you don't talk to her like that."

Behind him he could hear Christine saying something to the girl, who then let out an incredulous gasp. She hurried through the room, grabbed her purse off the sectional, and headed for the door. As she passed Tim she gave him a disgusted look and said "I can't believe you said you weren't married!" Tim grabbed for her, professing his innocence, but Mark held him by the collar of his ostentatiously pattered shirt and held him back until she was out the door.

"This is bullshit," he sputtered, and Mark just shrugged and tightened his grip. Tim flailed his arms arms as he tried to pull free but then Henry sidled up next to Mark, hand up and flipping a coin around his fingers as if he was also the other kind of magician.

"It's okay, Tim," Henry said, and his voice made Mark shudder. "You're okay. Why don't you calm down?"

Tim's thrashing subsided and he looked at Henry with a dazed and wondrous expression. "Yeah, okay. That's tight."

"Very tight," Henry nodded in agreement. He glanced over at Mark and he relaxed his grip on the little douchebag's shirt. "Now that your date's over, why don't you go see a movie or two? We'll have this place all squared away by the time you come back."

"For sure," Tim nodded, and Mark was convinced he could let go without him throwing a tantrum. Tim wavered unsteadily on his feet and started to move toward the front door, but then stopped and shook his head a little. "I should clean up," he said, looking back at Henry. "That steak was mad expensive."

"Sure thing," Henry said, pocketing his coin. Tim shuffled down the short hallway to their left, which led to the back of the house and, presumably, the kitchen and dining room.

"Must come in handy," Mark said as they followed Tim from a distance.

"Once or twice," Henry said.

Martin stopped them at a barely noticeable door halfway down the hall. "This is it," he said, pointing at it but keeping his distance. As he got near, Mark felt a sudden and oppressive heat close around him like a fist, nearly baking the air in his lungs.

"You okay?" Christine said, putting a hand on his arm.

"You don't feel that?" Mark said.

"What is it?" Henry asked.

"It's hot," Mark said, licking his desiccated lips. "Real hot."

Henry nodded and said "Get ready. It's probably going to get worse before it gets better."

"Story of my life," Mark said, steadying himself against the wall. Henry put his hand on the doorknob, and Mark expected him to draw back in pain from the heat. Henry gave him a look and Mark nodded, bracing himself. Henry opened the door and a thick burning smell and blast of dry heat hit him in the face. The others recoiled, clearly smelling it now. Mark gagged but kept himself under control, despite knowing what the rancid meat smell was.

"Oh my God," Christine said, covering her nose.

"That's definitely gotten worse," Martin said, fanning himself. "It wasn't this bad, or this hot, before."

"It's getting worse," Tim said, appearing behind them and still wearing his eerily chilled-out expression. "I think something died down there."

"No shit," Mark mumbled.

Henry patted Tim on the shoulder and gave him a slight push toward the front door. "It's okay, we'll take it from here."

"Tight," Tim said, walking past them. "Oh wait," he said, stopping as he passed behind Mark. "There was something else."

Mark looked over his shoulder and he saw the knife in Tim's hand a second before he stabbed it into Mark's side.

"How do you like the new place, Justin?" he growled in Mark's ear.

Chapter Eight

Martin and Christine screamed in unison.

Tim yanked the three inch steak knife, which must have been tucked up his sleeve, out of Mark's side, sending blood arcing across Christine. She recoiled, her lower back slamming painfully into the narrow table behind her and sending some of the assorted knickknacks and family pictures to the floor. Tim shoved Mark into Henry and the two of them stumbled, trying to keep their balance.

Martin lunged at Tim with a strained battle-cry, hooking an arm around Tim's before he could stab Mark again. Tim pulled free and elbowed Martin in the face, who made a different kind of cry as he fell back. Mark looked up from his now very red side just in time to raise an arm and stop the knife as it swung down at him. The surprising amount of force behind the slice was enough to push Mark back even more and leave a long gash across his forearm as he and Henry fell to the floor.

Tim turned his attention to her with a familiar feral grin. "Well look wh--"

Christine reached behind her, blindly grabbed something off the table, and smashed it against the side of Tim's head.

The something was a heavy picture frame and the glass shattered, leaving tiny cuts across the side of Tim's face and sending him staggering into the wall. As whatever was in his mind tried to process what was happening, she grabbed for the knife. Tim came to his senses and tried to push her away, but she was clamped down on his wrist. She slammed it, and her own hands, against the wall and the knife fell from Tim's grasp. She kicked it away, but turning away from Tim allowed him to grab a handful of her hair and yank her head back around to face him.

He snarled at her, and he had the same rabid look in his eye Mark did when he'd had her in a similar position. "You--"

She kneed him in the stomach and whatever misogynistic bullshit he was going to say was replaced by all the air rushing out of him. He let go of her hair and she swung an elbow into the injured side of his face, giving her enough room to raise a leg and kick him onto the floor.

Before he could get to his feet, Christine dropped down, pinning his right arm with her knee and then punching him in the head as much and as fast as she could with both fists.

"Whoa, whoa!" Martin said, waving his hands in front of her face around the ninth or tenth hit. "There's still a guy in there!"

Christine stopped, catching her breath. Tim's head fell to the side, and his face was already beginning to swell. He let out a weak groan and his eyelids fluttered then shut. Her knuckles were on fire, but she was thankful she remembered how to throw a punch without hurting her wrist. "Final girl rules," she said, catching her breath as she got off of Tim's chest. "Never stop attacking."

"I need some help!" Henry yelled from behind them.

He was kneeling next to Mark, glasses knocked off and pressing his wadded up jacket against Mark's side. Christine and Martin ran over, but stopped when they both realized panic was keeping them from knowing what to do.

"Towels," Henry said, trying to keep Mark from away from him in pain. "And belts or ties for straps."

"On it," Martin said, running to the stairs she'd glimpsed at the end of the hall. Christine followed but continued into the kitchen. Hand towels were in short supply but she grabbed as many as she could find, and then checked the freezer. She'd assumed correctly there'd be a bottle of vodka chilling there and brought it back with her too.

"Ah, shit," Mark said, realizing what the vodka was for.

"Good call," Henry nodded, taking the towels from her and pressing them against Mark's side. She knelt down, opened the bottle, and then poured some on the six-inch incision in his arm. She traded the bottle for one of the towels Henry was holding and wrapped it tightly around the wound.

"So unpleasant," Mark said, and then howled a string of obscenities through a clenched jaw as Henry poured vodka on his side. He'd been stabbed an inch or two below his rib cage, and it was pouring so much dark red blood it was either look away or start throwing up.

"I've got stuff!" Martin yelled, bounding down the stairs. He was clutching a bunch of belts in his hands and carrying an armload of bath towels. He dropped them at Henry's side and backed away. She was glad she wasn't the only freaked out by seeing so much blood.

Henry looked over at her and tilted his head down toward Mark. "Can you?" She swallowed hard and then nodded, taking over putting pressure on the wound as Henry and Martin laced together the belts.

"I told you this could be my last night on Earth," Mark chuckled weakly at her.

"Shut up," she said, pressing a little harder.

"I don't think it will be," Henry said from behind her. "It's deep but I don't think he hit anything vital."

"Oh good," Mark winced. "It only *feels* like I'm dying."

"Remember when I said it was going to get worse before it got better?" Henry said, coming back to Mark's side with a string of three belts tied together.

"I hate you," Mark said, and Henry nodded sympathetically.

They eased Mark onto folded bath towels and then wrapped the belts around them, cinching them so tightly Mark yelled until he was red in the face. Christine was both unnerved and thankful it seemed like Henry and Martin had done something like this before.

"I'll be right back," Henry said, heading over to Tim. Before Christine could ask, Henry knelt down and placed a hand on Tim's head. Henry closed his eyes and at first nothing happened, but then Tim began to twitch and let out little groans. When they faded, Henry stayed by him for a few moments before standing back up with a middle-aged grunt of exertion.

"That should both drive the presence out of him and make sure he stays asleep for a while."

"Great," Mark said, trying to sit up. "Now let's get this over with."

"The hell are you doing?" Christine said, pushing him back down, "You need to go to a hospital right now!"

"I'm not waiting to get this thing out of me. If it can get that guy then it can definitely get me, and I'm not going to wear charm bracelets for the rest of my life."

"Dude, come on," Martin said incredulously, and then looked to Henry for support.

He remained quiet.

"This guy gets it," Mark said, nodding in his direction. "We'll have to come up with a lot more bullshit to explain everything that's already happened, and if we leave coming back to try again will be even harder. And all while it's going to get stronger."

Christine looked at Henry, desperate for him to disagree. The look on Henry's face made it clear he wasn't going to.

"He's not wrong," Henry said. "We can still cover for this, although it won't exactly be easy."

"You heard the man," Mark said, struggling to get to his feet. "Uppy-ups."

She let go of Mark's hand and the guys pulled him to his feet, each supporting him under his arms. With Mark off the ground, the pool of his congealing blood looked huge. Slow rivers of it crawled along the wood floor, and when she stepped away from them her body started trembling. She hunched over, hands on her knees, trying to keep from vomiting everywhere. She wanted to believe it was the fight adrenaline wearing off, but she knew it had more to do with seeing another lake of blood in this deathtrap.

When she successfully defeated the urge, she looked back up at the other three who stared in concern.

"I'm fine," she lied, "but I...," she started, but couldn't bring herself to say it. This was too much, and whatever urge had driven her to make sure she saw this through was now a distant memory.

"It's okay," Henry said, watching her closely. "I can get him downstairs myself. You and Martin get Tim out of here, and then he'll come back for Mark."

"I'm fine," Mark said, face pale and beginning to shiver a bit. "Don't worry about me." She didn't have the heart to say not only did she not need his approval, but his safety wasn't foremost on her mind.

"Okay," she said, nodding in relief.

Martin helped them with the basement door while she moved away and back towards Tim. Another wave of meat-stench struck her, so strong she wanted to just bolt out the front door and not stop running until she was home. Mark looked back at her before they disappeared down the stairs and all she could think to do was give a weak wave and say "Good luck."

"Right, let's do this," Martin said, hurrying over to Tim. They bent down, each grabbing him under an armpit, and then lifted. Christine moved toward the front door but Martin stopped her.

"Backyard. Someone is absolutely going to call the cops if they see a passed out White guy on the front lawn."

"Fair enough," she said. "Is he going to be safe out there?"

"Yes?" Martin said through a forced smile. "At least, safer than he would be in here."

"Good enough for me."

Tim's knees dragged across the floor as they carried him to the sliding doors in the back, which led to a mostly concrete patio. They dragged Tim across it, along the stone path running through the plants and flowers and into the lush and expansive back yard.

"I can't believe you're friends with this guy," she said when they'd stopped to take a brief rest.

"I mean, not really?" Martin said, catching his breath. "But I was so starved for human contact I couldn't wait to come to his stupid party. I wondered why he'd invited me, but I guess this is why."

"What are you talking about?" she said as they picked Tim up again.

"A lot of the time magic things can get drawn together. People, places--"

"Things?"

He chuckled. "Yup. All the magic nouns can get drawn to each other in weird ways, and it's not until after the fact you realize you're just getting put where you're needed to be. Here's good." They lowered Tim down, having just enough strength left to make sure he didn't get dropped on his face.

"Are you saying it's God?" she said as they headed back.

"Who knows if it's *Hashem,* but I think there's got to be something on our side giving us a nudge now and then."

Christine was quiet, lost in thought as she worried about being pulled into more of this bullshit and not realizing until it was too late. Martin jogged to the patio, looking back as they reached the wooden fence separating yard from driveway.

"Go on," he said, waving toward the door in the fence. "I'll be right out."

She slowed a little, wondering if Martin would actually be able to drag Mark up the steps and out of the house on his own given how much trouble Tim's limp body had given them. She stamped down the urge to help, remembering the pool of blood on the ground, the past trauma, and the confirmed presence of demons, and hurried toward the fence.

Just after she reached the stone path leading to the fence door her foot hit something and she tripped. She fell forward, but her foot was stuck, so she just teetered off-balance on one leg. Looking back she saw her shoe was caught on something in the mulch between the stones.

Before she could pull away, whatever held on to her foot pulled so hard her other leg skidded out from under her and she fell on her side. There was another tug on her leg and she scooted back with her free leg and elbows. There was an eruption of soft earth as she retreated, dragging whatever held her out of the ground.

It was a half burned, half skeletal kid clutching her ankle with its tiny, rotted hands. His body was cut in half at the waist and it pulled itself closer with its free hand.

She screamed and tried to shake it off. Soil tumbled away, revealing more gray and rotted skin, empty eye sockets, and lipless mouth.

"Welcome back, lady," it said in a voice sounding like something from Little Rascals. "I never got to play with girls before," it said. "But I'm going to have so much fu--"

"Not today!" Martin said, landing with both feet on the tiny back and then stomping on its head and giving her a chance to pull free. "Go!" he yelled at her over the crunch of tiny bones and the thing's screeching. She didn't need to be told twice.

She only made it a couple more steps toward the fence before something else burrowed up from the ground in front of her. It was another dirt-covered child's body, equally rotted and burned, but with limbs broken in multiple places, strings of flesh just barely keeping them together.

"Eric's a creep," the girl-thing hissed. "I just want to make you one of my dollies." Christine backed up.

"Hold on!" Martin yelled, giving Eric a final stomp before rushing over to her. He drew his leg back to kick the girl-thing out of Christine's path, but as he swung she folded in on herself, the multiple joints dropping her flat to the ground in an instant. Martin's kick went right over it, and as he tried to recover its limbs uncoiled and it was standing again. It jumped up, grabbed Martin's shirt, and tugged him to the ground.

The thing swung its floppy arms down on Martin, battering at his head while he tried to protect himself. Christine grabbed one of the metal patio chairs and swung it into the thing, knocking it off Martin's chest. As he stood up a fist-sized rock struck him in the small of the back and he shouted in surprise and pain.

"We ain't done playin' yet, lady!" The thing called 'Eric' rolled toward them, dried and broken bones clicking together like a sack of marbles. On the next rotation of its torso it threw another rock, this one coming within an inch of Christine's face.

"Strike!" Another rotten boy child called out from their right. This one was decayed but not burnt, with a cut through its neck so deep its head was held on by just a few strands of flesh. It had a shovel gripped in both hands and stalked toward them faster than the other two seemed capable of. "My turn at bat!" it yelled, swinging the shovel at them in a sweeping arc. Christine pulled Martin back and it just barely missed him.

Once he regained his balance, Martin pushed Christine behind him. "Hold on," he said, holding his arms out in front of him. He took a deep breath, but before he could do anything another rock struck him in the side and he yelled in pain.

Shovel Boy scurried forward and swung again, pushing them back to the house. To their left Broken Girl shuffled toward them, and in front of them Eric the Half Kid picked up another rock and hurled it at them.

"Inside!" Martin said, ducking it. She slid the glass door open and closed just as the shovel smacked into it, spreading a network of cracks through the glass. The two of them backed away, waiting for another swing, but the nearly-headless Shovel Boy just stared at them and smiled, tapping the glass.

"Out the front it is," Martin said, gesturing behind him while keeping his eyes on the glass door. "Go, I'll keep an eye on them."

Christine turned back to the hallway and caught sight again of the lake of blood filling the hallway. She turned and headed through the dining room and into the living room. It may be the longer route, but she wasn't about to try to tip toe through or jump over it. If she got any more blood on her she wasn't sure she'd be able to function.

Halfway through the living room a deafening burst of static erupted from the speakers surrounding her, and she jumped and covered her ears. Martin yelled something from the back of the house, but the static was so loud it felt like a physical thing shaking her body. The massive television on the wall came to life, the screen filling with digital noise and distortion, and then the fireplace roared to life, flames spitting at her from across the room.

She made it a few more steps before sparks shot out the speaker right above her head, making her jump back. The static was abruptly replaced by over-powering electric guitar riffs and a bone-rattling beat.

"Fuck's sake," Christine said, registering what song it was. Martin hurried into the room, a look of confusion on his face as he tried to figure out what was happening.

"Is that--" he started, but as the words to the song started they were joined by a mocking voice echoing down from the chimney.

"What's somebody like you doing in a place like this?"

A pair of heavily burned hands reached out from the inside the chimney at the top of the fireplace, curling around to grab the mantle.

"Did you come alone or did you bring all your friends?"

An equally cooked head dropped into view, the flames behind shining through the hole plowed through its skull.

"This fucking guy," Martin said.

"This *fucking* guy," Christine snarled.

Out of the corner of her eye she saw the nearly headless terror come around the corner and make a beeline towards the distracted Martin, shovel clutched in both hands like a baseball bat.

"Look out!" she hollered over the music. It was loud enough, and Martin jumped into the living room just as Shovel Boy caved in part of the wall where his head had been.

Christine ran for the front door, but Shovel Boy's distraction gave Jack enough time to pull himself from the chimney and tumble into her path. He leisurely rose to his full height, shaking his arms and legs in time with the music as if to stretch whatever muscles were left on him.

"What's somebody like you doing in a place like this?" he sang again, a mean smile spreading across what was left of his face. The tempo of the song picked up, and Jack lunged toward her, grabbing a thin metal floor lamp along the way.

"Oh, Christiney," he yelled, swinging the lamp at her. "I've waited so long for this!"

Behind her she heard the impact of shovel against wall, and she glanced back just in time to avoid running right into Martin. They both retreated, Jack and Shovel Boy each blocking one of the exits at the far ends of the large room. With the heat of the fireplace bearing down on them, all they could do was move closer to the giant sectional in the middle of the room.

The two monsters came at them from opposite sides, swinging their makeshift weapons almost in time with the beat. Christine vaulted over the back of the couch just before Jack could cave her skull in with the heavy base of the lamp. Martin made it most of the way over as well, but his foot dipped into the space between cushions and Shovel Boy hit him in the side. Martin fell awkwardly to the floor, gasping in pain, and Shovel Boy leapt down at him.

Jack vaulted on to the back of the sofa, swinging the lamp back and forth to block either direction she could run in. "Fitting soundtrack, hmm?" His head moved as if he was winking at her with his missing eye. "Darren always sang that stupid old song, so maybe this'll be my jam." He grabbed the lamp in both hands, raised it above his head, and jumped at her.

She ran, unable to get to the front door but able to put a recliner between them. Jack cackled in laughter as he jumped first on, then over it, driving her further back to the billowing flames of the fireplace.

Something popped up from behind the couch and where she'd last seen Martin. It arced high, almost hitting the ceiling fan, and then bounced off the coffee table and onto the floor. Jack turned to look and she jumped forward, grabbing the end of the lamp and tried to pull it from his grasp. He kept his grip and she found herself in a tug-of-war with it until Jack let go and let her fall on her ass.

"Woooooooooon't let you get awaaaaaaaayyyyyyyy," he sang along, stepping on his end of the lamp so she couldn't pick it up.

"Hey!" Martin yelled. "Leave Katy Perry out of this." He charged forward, shovel out in front of him like a spear. Jack turned just enough for Martin to stab it in the chest, the momentum pushing it into the wall and pinning him there.

"Motherfucker!" Jack screeched, reaching out and swiping at Martin but unable to reach him. Holding the end of the shovel with one hand, Martin raised the other and closed his eyes. The atmosphere around Christine changed to something akin to a storm about to sweep in. Jack, instead of clawing at Martin, grabbed the shovel and pulled itself forward. It slid up the handle a couple of inches and reached out for Martin's hand. Just before they touched, blue sparks arced between Martin's fingers and Jack was pushed back hard against the wall, the arm it had been reaching out with crushed against its chest.

Jack made muffled gurgling sounds and Martin moved closer to him, the invisible force from his hand crushing the thing against the wall like a trash compactor. Martin's face was red with exertion but he pressed forward until what was left of Jack's skull imploded and the rest of him crumbled into dust on the floor. As he did, there was another quick burst of static and the music mercifully stopped.

Martin straightened up and wiped the sweat from his brow. "How'd that taste, asshole?" he said between gasps of breath.

Martin dropped to one knee, gasping for breath. Before Christine could try to help him up, she heard the pattering of running feet coming towards her. She turned and saw the now completely headless boy's body tottering toward them unsteadily. Christine yanked the shovel out of the wall, spun around, and smacked the thng into the roaring fireplace. It twitched and hissed, and from across the room she could hear the high pitched squeals coming from its head.

The headless and now flaming body tried to crawl out of the fireplace but Christine pinned it in there with the tip of the shovel. "Taste what?" she said, glancing in Martin's direction.

"You had to be there," he said, walking across the room. "But also, what the hell was up with that song?"

"You don't want to know," she said. The flames had died down from supernatural inferno levels and were now coming almost entirely from the still twitching flaming child's body. Across the room, Martin bent down and carefully picked up Shovel Boy's head by one of its remaining tufts of hair.

Martin walked over, head shrieking high-pitched obscenities. "Fair enough. Besides," he tossed the head into the fire, where it immediately burst into flame. "'Teenage Dream' is her best work anyway."

When she was sure the child-thing had stopped moving she let the shovel drop to the ground. "Is that it?" she asked, looking around for the next nightmare to come leaping out at her.

"Should be," Martin said, guiding her toward the front door. "I gave Jack the old 'Get thee behind me douchebag,' so he won't be giving us any more troubles. Now let's get you--"

He was interrupted by a bellowing scream from beneath them.

Chapter Nine

Mark swore with every stair they stepped down. His arm was around Henry's shoulders, although Henry was a little too short for it to be comfortable. With every step the hole in his side moved and introduced him to a new kind of pain. When they reached the bottom, Henry lowered Mark on to his back as gently as he could, which still felt like he was being ripped open. The basement was vastly different now, and everything Mark had envied as a kid. There was a huge home theater set-up, arcade cabinet, and even a pool table. The unlit neon beer and pot-leaf signs, as well as the excessive amounts of "tastefully nude" photography, did wonders for curbing his envy. Mark craned his neck up to look at the far wall where the furnace used to be, but the area was blocked by a new wood-paneled wall with a single door in the middle.

He let his head fall back to the floor, trying to let the makeover fool him into thinking he wasn't bleeding out on the same ground so many others had before. With effort, Henry sat cross-legged next to him, rolled up the sleeves of his dress shirt, and then studied the room.

"This is bad," Henry said.

"Yeah," Mark said. "Who uses wood paneling nowadays?"

Henry gave him a wry smile. "You know that's not what I meant, but you're not wrong." He took a deep breath and reached into his bag. "This place is radiating a lot more demonic energy than I was expecting."

"God forbid anything be easy."

"In this line of work, you learn to be adaptable," Henry said. He took a small, golden statue out of the bag, held it out in front of him with both hands, closed his eyes for a few seconds, and then placed it in front of him. Mark was going to ask what it was, but he was hit with the overwhelming but familiar smell of smoke and charred meat.

Human meat, you mean. How many people can say they can recognize the difference?

Mark gritted his teeth and tried his deep breathing exercises, but with every inhale he could taste the burning air tinged with cooked blood.

"I think you're making it mad," Mark said.

"Good." Henry placed a hand on Mark's chest. "You ready?"

"As I'll ever be, Doc." Henry closed his eyes and Mark did likewise.

A heat rushed through his body, and Mark thought the furnace flames had caught up to him, but these were soothing and peaceful, like being wrapped in a warm blanket. He had the sensation of floating, and when he opened his eyes he realized he was standing up and the pain in his side was gone.

The refurbished basement was gone too, having returned to the decayed and bare state of ten years ago, complete with cracked cement floor, wooden beams overhead with dangling chains, and an oppressive dry heat snuffing out any sense of comfort. The furnace was back as well, in all its black-iron glory, with pipes snaking out from the top like an upside-down spider. In the front was the two-foot square door to the fuel chamber, and through the dirty glass window in the middle he could see the flames roiling and hungry.

"It's okay," Henry said from behind him, putting a hand on Mark's shoulder.

"Not even remotely," Mark said, turning around to face him. Over Henry's shoulder he could see the rickety wooden stairs in the same place as the ones they'd descended minutes before. Underneath them was the makeshift metal cage where the children had been kept before being tortured and made to see the furnace's demonic resident.

The one you built. The one you kept them in.

Mark jumped and spun around. That wasn't just "negative self-talk," it was whispered in his ear in a rush of hot, smoke-filled air.

"It's okay," Henry said, turning Mark to face him and placing his other hand on Mark's shoulder. "It's not going to go without a fight, but I'm here with you."

Mark nodded, and smoke began to seep out of Henry's eyes like tears. Before Mark could say anything, he felt something moving against his shoulders as if something was squirming under the skin of Henry's palms. "What is--" Mark started, but Henry closed his eyes and shook his head.

"Don't worry about it," Henry said, his voice deeper and with a slight echo to it. "This is...perfectly normal."

"You have a fucked up version of normal," Mark said, and then Henry turned him back around to face the furnace.

"You have no idea," Henry said. "But that'll get us through this. Hang on, this is going to be uncomfortable."

You're used to that, aren't you?

He swatted at the air next to his ear.

"Fuck off," Mark whispered. The heat exuding from the furnace was making him drip sweat, and his chest clenched when he realized this was what Corwin's victims felt before their gruesome ends.

Your victims, buddy. Let's not forget that, hmm?

Mark started to say something but the clenching pain in his chest magnified, sucking all the air out of his lungs and making him drop to his knees. Henry's hands didn't leave his shoulders, and whatever was under his palms wriggled around even more. Just when he thought he was going to pass out, the pain relented and he was able to breathe again.

"It's okay," Henry said from behind with his double-voice. "This is what we want."

There was a screech of metal and the door on the furnace swung open. Flames poured out into the room, and Mark winced at the unnaturally bright fire inside.

Ah, come on, Justin. That was your whole thing, wasn't it? Make them see what was in the fire and all? Don't pussy out of it.

"Get out of my head," Mark snarled, shutting his eyes and focusing on where the damn voice was coming from.

I can't get out! I'm YOU, remember? The psychopath child-murderer who took the pussy way out! It's not going to be so easy now, kiddo, that's for damn sure!

"I know you're not me," Mark said. "You're just evil stuck to Justin's soul."

And how do you figure that?

"Because you never called yourself 'I' before."

The pain in his chest rose again, but this time he was ready for it. He could now feel the thing inside clenching against his heart. Mark grabbed at his chest as if he could tear it open and pull the poisoning thing right out.

"There you go," Henry said. "You got th--"

Henry's voice cut off and his hands disappeared from Mark's shoulders. He swayed, almost falling forward, and the pain in his chest shifted to his stab wound. Mark opened his eyes, confirming he was back in the frat basement. The only change was the heavy pounding of bass shaking the lights hanging from the ceiling. Next to him Henry lay on his side, glasses knocked off and eyes closed. Someone stepped over him and stood over Mark, a pool cue held casually in his hand. The light on the ceiling behind him blocked his features, but he could see light coming through a hole in his head.

Not his head, he realized, but his neck.

"Hey buddy," the wheezing but familiar voice said. "Look at you, all grown up."

He knelt down, sitting on Mark's chest with his knees on either side of him. He leaned forward, the remnants of long hair hanging in front of its burned face, and pressed the pool cue down across Mark's throat.

"We've got a lot to catch up on, huh?" Steve, his high school best friend, said.

The same best friend he'd killed in this basement.

***

Henry knew hurrying was a rookie mistake, but he thought he'd be quick enough to exorcise Mark before going on the offensive.

"It's been nearly a year since you've been out on a case. A real one," Monica had told him before he left. "Not since Lexie got hurt, so I want you to promise to take it easy and be careful, okay? You may be a little out of practice." He brushed it off, mostly so she wouldn't worry, but as it was with most things she was right. The pain in the back of his head was bad, but the realization he'd broken a promise and was going to have to explain another head wound to his wife stung more.

He pushed himself up onto an elbow and saw Mark next to him, a burnt teenager sitting on his chest and crushing his throat with a pool cue. Mark's legs kicked as he tried to push it off, but he wasn't having much luck.

Henry reached out, but something grabbed his wrist and yanked him back. It pulled him up off the ground for a second and then he crashed down on his back. A young man loomed over him, but unlike Mark's attacker he wasn't burned. His was shirt unbuttoned, revealing a long scar from lower hip up to the opposite shoulder.

"Not so fast," it said. "Those two have a score to settle."

Henry tried to pull his arm free, but his head was still swimming and his limbs weren't doing what they were told. This was Darren, he realized, the one who'd controlled Mark's body a decade ago and had willingly sacrificed himself for the demon. Darren grabbed the scar at the center of its chest with the free hand, dug the fingers deep into the flesh, and pulled. The scar ripped open like a zipper and a cloud of thick black smoke descended down over Henry's face.

He tried to wave it away, but the smoke thickened and then held his arm in tentacle-like strands. He could feel the solidifying smoke gather around his head, and even though he kept his eyes and mouth shut it pushed against them and tried to force its way inside.

"In the meantime," it said. "I'm going to add a few more souls to the roster."

***

Mark could barely keep the cue up long enough to catch his breath, and every time he got it up Steve dug his heel into the stab wound on Mark's side.

"Hurts, huh?" Steve said, mouth moving but the sound coming from the off-center hole in his neck. "I hope it's as much as it did when I was bleeding out on the floor over there. Do you know how long it took me to die, Mark? Five minutes, at least. Five minutes of drowning in my own blood while you just watched me. I died looking at your stupid fucking face, you little pansy." He finished the sentence by jabbing his heel into him with every word.

"You're not Steve," Mark said, straining so hard to breathe he couldn't tell if he was audible.

"You wish," Steve snarled. "I remember wiping away your tears and comforting you every time you got too 'stressed' or 'freaked out,' which seemed to be every other goddamn day. How much of my very short life did I waste on your bullshit? Too goddamn much, that's for sure."

"He was my friend," Mark said, anger helping him find a reserve of strength. "I may have been a crybaby...but Steve was at least funny about it."

"Oh, you want funny Steve?" it said, smiling wider than he'd have been able to without the burns and rot. "This one's a riot." Steve gestured upward with his head.

"The third in our love triangle is upstairs right now, and Jack is having a good time with her. She's going to be hurt a lot, and then

I get to take a turn." Steve leaned forward, pressing more weight against Mark's throat and lowering its face right above his.

"I can't wait to absolutely impale 'ol Christine. And I mean that in *every* way." It laughed, and Mark winced at the puffs of fetid air blowing from the ragged hole in its throat. "And there's nothing you or the diversity-hire over there can do about it."

Mark looked and saw Darren standing over Henry, dark smoke oozing out of his chest and crushing Henry like a squirming mass of pythons.

"And when we're done with all of them, we're gonna to take turns crawling up inside you and make you do the most heinous shit imaginable. And this time, you're going to be awake for all of it."

Chapter Ten

Henry shook his head back and forth, trying to keep the smoky tendrils from forcing their way into his unprotected nostrils and ears.

"You really thought you could just walk in here and face our God? That He hasn't harvested enough souls to defend Himself? Who do you think you are?"

"Not the one to test, that's for damn sure," Henry growled through clenched teeth. He balled his hands into fists and he could feel his insides building up heat and power. "I've got my own furnace."

Darren looked confused for a second, and then its eyes opened wide in surprise as the clouds around Henry's arm and face began to burn away. Darren let go of Henry's arm, but now it was Henry's turn to hold on.

"I don't think so," Henry said. Darren had backed up enough for Henry to plant a foot against its lower stomach. Bearing down, he pushed with his foot while pulling with his arm. Darren tried to shake free but Henry's grip was so tight he could feel what passed for bones begin to crack under the pressure. Henry felt the thing's torso snap and tear with the opposing pressure, and Darren's sustained scream of agony echoed off the walls around them. The last of whatever was holding it together snapped and tor in half along the path of the scar. The lower half of its body was kicked across the room and the top half swung over Henry's head and hit the ground behind him with a solid, wet thump.

Henry struggled to his feet, keeping his grip as Darren tried to pull itself away with its other hand. Henry stepped on what was left of its chest, and then fire roared down the thing's captured arm. Darren screeched and writhed as the flames quickly spread to its torso. Unbothered by the heat, Henry raised his foot and stomped down on the flaming skull, shattering it. The screaming ceased, and the rest of its body twisted and burned until all that was left were crispy piles of ash. Henry let go of the arm and it crumbled onto the ground.

"Holy shit," said Martin from the stairs behind him.

Henry turned and saw Martin and Christine were almost to the bottom of the stairs, looking from him to the struggling Mark with equal amount of shock. Henry could feel the power he'd let loose swirling around him, and judging by the way Martin was transfixed he could see it to. Not ideal, but not the immediate problem.

The thing on Mark's chest looked over its shoulder at Christine and let out as good of a wolf-whistle as it could with a hole through the neck. "Aren't you a sight for sore eyes," it said. "Let me finish here and we can pick up where we left off."

"Enough," Henry snapped.

The thing turned to look just in time for Henry to palm its rotting face. It dropped the pool cue and grabbed Henry's wrist with both hands, but Henry's fingers dug deep into the ruined skin and scorched bone. There was a hiss of flesh sizzling, and then white flame burst out of its eyes and neck hole. Henry pushed forward and slammed the back of its head against the floor, where it exploded in a flash of fire and ash. The rest of it twitched and then dissolved into smoke.

Mark sucked in massive gulps of air, and Martin and Christine rushed to his side. Henry reigned in the magical energy rippling through his body and knelt next to Mark's head.

Mark glared up at him. "This plan is really going great. I'm excited I'm a part of it."

"It's going about as good as they usually do," Martin muttered. Henry shot him a look but Martin didn't make eye contact.

"We can still do this," Henry said, placing a hand on Mark's forehead and diving back into his mind.

***

"Jesus," Mark said between coughs. "Why does my throat still hurt in here?"

They were back in the original murder basement, and Mark was doubled over and Henry next to him with a hand on his shoulder.

"It's a projection," Henry said. "Metaphysical stuff we don't have time for. You ready to try again?"

"Go for it," Mark hacked, straightening up. The coughing had taken his mind off of Steve's ghost or whatever trying to kill him, and he knew he should've mentally prepared for the possibility. Steve's death here, while an accident, was still Mark's fault no matter how hard he tried not to think about it.

You did it to yourself, man. Have you tried not *killing your loved ones?*

Henry's hand gripped Mark's shoulder harder and he felt the thing in his chest squirming again. Mark bore down and he could feel it being forced up into his throat.

"I'm so goddamn sick of you," he said, right before his airway was painfully blocked. He heaved, trying to force whatever it was up and out. It buzzed and shook like an angry beehive, and then tiny, sharp things grabbed on to his back teeth and dug into his soft palate. Mark opened wide and reached deep into his mouth to grab it. It was hard and cold, and tried to pull itself away, but Mark grabbed onto one of the protrusions with his thumb and forefinger and started to pull.

It came out of his mouth, scraping against his tongue and teeth as it thrashed. Mark grabbed what already emerged with both hands and pulled. Feelers kicked and scratched against his nose and chin as it fought him. For a moment he thought it was going to be like some evil, never-ending magician's scarves, but when his arms were fully extended it popped out of his mouth.

Nearly three feet long and pitch black, it shifted from feeling soft and dough-like to hard and chitinous, like insect's shell. As it tried to free itself, little multi-jointed legs formed and then were drawn back in at a frantic pace.

"There you go," Henry said from behind him.

Mark cocked his arm back, turned, and hurled the thing at the furnace. It hit about a foot above the fuel chamber door, but the thick metal crumbled like he'd thrown a boulder. Flame spouted from the cracks, and the maze of pipes overhead burst open with black steam.

Mark flinched away and closed his eyes for a second, and when he opened them he was back in reality. The others had their hands on his arms and shoulders, trying to keep him still as he tried to sit up and expel the phantom object from his throat. He waved them away and was reminded of the knife would in his side.

"Back up, back up," he said, trying to speak as loud as he could.

"No time," Henry said. "You guys need to go."

Christine and Martin got on either side of Mark and helped him to his feet. They were taller than Henry so it was easier to step along with them as they climbed the stairs, but it was twice as painful as the descent had been. He could feel blood dripping down his side, the straps holding the towels in place having been loosened with all the attempted murder. There was a rumbling from underneath them, and Mark looked over his shoulder just before his line of sight was blocked at the first landing. A crack had appeared on the floor, right where Mark had been laying, and an angry red glow was shining from it.

"I don't recommend looking back," Martin said.

"I'm pretending this isn't even happening," Christine said.

Mark hoped he'd get there one day, but he severely doubted it.

***

"Show yourself," Henry commanded, voice reverberating around the room with magical authority.

The ground shook again and another crack appeared in the floor. Henry backed up, loosening his hold on the power within him and readying to strike. Dark smoke like what had poured forth from Darren began to seep up from the cracks, and as the cloud obscured the ground there was another small quake. Henry held out his hand, ready to burn away whatever emerged, but something dropped from the ceiling and on to his arm.

It was the top half of a burned child, clawing and biting at his arm. He shook it to get the thing off, but then something skittered at him from the side and crashed into his bad knee. He buckled, but was able to remain upright as the multi-jointed corpse of an equally young girl wrapped itself around his leg, trying to pull him even more off balance.

"How dare you come to our neighborhood? Into my house!" a man's voice growled from behind, and two sets of arms reached around him, grabbing his torso and trying to wrap around his neck. The angles of the arms were all wrong and glancing back he could see it was a man and woman's body parts mashed together into a single abomination. The man's head was at Henry's shoulder, but the woman's was down by his side and just under his arm.

"My son! You killed my son!" it shrieked before biting into Henry's side. They were Corwin's parents, Henry realized, clearly unaware of who actually dismembered them. The weight drove Henry down onto his bad knee as they continued to pummel, scratch, and bite him. The black smoke swirled around his ankles, and he could make out clicking and scraping sounds inside over the racial epithets the corpses hissed at him.

"Enough," Henry snapped. A torrent of magic burst through him as he stood. Flesh popped and burned behind him as wings of flame burst from his back and right through what had become of Mr. and Mrs. Corwin. They fell to the ground, reduced to cinders. He grabbed the half a boy clinging to his arm, raised it in the air, and then smashed it into the girl clinging to his leg over and over again until it tumbled to the ground in a heap. Henry raised the torso in the air again and smashed the two together again, this time with a burst of flame.

"Is that the best you can do?" Henry screamed, his voice only half his. The wings on his back rose and then swept down, blowing the smoke around his feet back to where it had emerged. As it retreated, multiple insect-like legs and crustacean-esque claws scurried back to where they could hide again.

There was another rumble from the ground, and the clacking of claws and legs grew in volume as solid black clouds rose from the cracks like ink floating in water.

You dare, it snapped in Henry's mind. *I will devour your entire existence! I will shred your soul into--*

"You're not doing shit," Henry said. He strode forward and plunged both arms elbow deep into the swirling column of darkness. It squealed in surprise as Henry grabbed the first solid thing he could find and started to squeeze. The fire that erupting from his hands burned away the darkness, reaveling the outline of the maggot-shaped thing covered in legs, claws, and feelers. The top of it plunged down around Henry's upper body and circled him, lashing out with its multitude of appendages.

I will bury myself in you and make you my instrument, it cried out in Henry's mind, full of desperation.

A rumbling rose up from Henry's core. *This one is claimed,* a voice deep inside Henry roared. *And you are nothing before me, you weak little insect.*

It wailed in agony as Henry's hands began to rend and twist the center of its form. The remaining darkness was pulled down into his grip, and what was wrapped around him drew back as well. Henry gathered it in his hands like he was violently crumbling paper into a ball, and when he had its essence compacted down to a single handful the room shuddered and pulsed around him. Even as just an irregular wad of darkness about the size of a golf ball it still tried to slip between his fingers and escape.

I think not.

Before he realized what was happening, Henry's head tilted back and he dropped the thing into his open mouth. It fell through Henry's essence with a painful flash of cold and then it vanished. He doubled over and coughed for a few seconds, hoping something would come out, but there was nothing coming back up. He stood and pulled back the fire he'd let loose, slamming doors shut in his mind.

"That was disgusting," Henry said, wiping his mouth with the back of his hand. "Don't ever pull that crap again."

The room was silent, and then his stomach grumbled loudly.

Chapter Eleven

The waiting room in the nicer of the two hospitals in Cedar Ridge had been remodeled, so that was nice. Christine was grateful she didn't have to stare at the same ugly paint she had the last time she'd been here, waiting to find out if her father was going to die and processing that her brother already had. The paint was still ugly, and Mark was going to live, but there was plenty of other stuff to ponder and worry about.

Henry had emerged from the house after a nerve-wracking amount of time. She'd wanted to take Mark to get checked out immediately but he'd insisted they wait until Henry came out.

When he did and said it was over, she felt a rush of relief unlike anything she'd felt before, although Henry warned them "now comes the hard part." They retrieved Tim from the backyard, woke him, and Henry "explained" what had happened. It was a simple case of an old friend bringing people by to take care of weird plumbing issues in the basement, but then a bunch of them took an unfortunate tumble down the stairs while holding tools carelessly. Whatever Henry did was effective, and they loaded Tim and Mark into the Jeep. Christine asked how they were going to account for all the damage, but Henry told her they would take care of it while she took the other two to the hospital.

The bored resident who stitched Mark up seemed to buy the story, as Tim was quite expressive about it, but the nurse working with him clearly did not. She gave Christine a look and when she nodded in an "I'm fine and not in danger" manner, the nurse replied with a "guess it's none of my business if two idiots get in a fight and one of them stabs the other" shrug. While upset over the whole thing, whatever Henry had done to Tim kept him from wanting to press any charges or get the police involved.

Mark was admitted for observation, wanting to make sure he didn't take a turn for the worse in the night and require a splenectomy. She grudgingly decided to cancel her flight and try to get another one once she knew Mark was going to be okay, and she opted for some alone time while he lay in the hallway waiting for a room. She'd reached peak doom-scrolling when Henry walked over with a couple of cans of soda and two bags of suspiciously generic "party mix."

"That seemed a little fast for home repair," she said, taking the offered snacks.

"It may surprise you," he said, "but we have ways to make it go faster."

"I bet. Where's your sidekick? I need to thank him for saving my ass."

Henry chuckled. "He insisted he was fine, so I dropped him at home. I wanted him to come get looked at, but he's still on his parent's insurance and he didn't want them to find out he'd gotten hurt."

She shook her head. "Kids these days."

He smiled, and then asked how she was doing.

"Seriously questioning my sanity, and not just from fending off a dead teenager while dance music was playing. Or seeing Steve.. .like that."

"Those kinds of things are never easy," Henry nodded. "The thing to remember, especially in circumstances like this, is that it wasn't really those people. Just warped echoes of what they once were."

"Well that clears it up, " she snickered.

"I know, easier said than done for sure. And believe me, I've had to be reminded on a few occasions."

There was a lull as they both crunched away at their dinners, and then Henry spoke up again.

"You said that wasn't why you're questioning your sanity. May I ask what is?"

"Such a gentleman." She thought about it and then said, "I'd reached a point in my life where I really thought I'd put all this stuff to rest. I'd packed it away, cried about it, journaled about it, and was done. But I still came all the way out here, hooked up with the guy from the worst relationship I've ever had, and *voluntarily* went into a place I knew was literally filled with ghosts. It's so stupid."

Henry nodded solemnly. "I'm sorry about that, I really am. I was worried calling you was too much pressure, and I should've known better than to be so...persistent." He was either using magical acting tricks or legitimately holding back tears. "I honestly think you were what got Mark to help us, and if he hadn't this would have ended up a lot worse."

"I wish I could say I was glad I did my part."

"I shouldn't have let you come inside. I could've...I *should've* pushed back harder, and it almost got you really hurt."

She nodded, not wanting to think about how many brushes with death she'd had in the past twenty-four hours. "It was my own stupid fault. One last crazy push so I could go home and really know it's done." She looked over at him. "And you're *sure* it's done, right?"

"As done as it can be," Henry said. "It's not trapped in something like before, it's been banished back to whatever hell it came from."

"Good," she said, not wanting to address the concept of multiple hells. "And the people it...ate, or whatever, they're free? In heaven or something?"

"Or something," Henry said. "There's not a definitive answer, but they're wherever they need to be."

"Good for them," she said. She took a drink and added, "Earlier Martin said magic stuff is attracted to people who've already experienced it. Is that true?"

Henry nodded. "In a sense. Those people tend to find themselves in these kinds of situations more often."

"Is there some sort of whammy or magic rock you can give me to keep them as far away as possible? Twice in almost thirty years is enough."

He smiled a little. "You should be okay."

"I want more than 'should,'" she said. "I don't want to just cross my fingers and hope I don't buy a haunted car or discover my next Tinder match is a vampire."

"Be careful on there anyway, but I'll tell you what I've told my kids about avoiding this stuff, and that's to trust your gut."

The look she gave him made him nod apologetically. "I know," he said. "It sounds dumb, but it's true. Those hunches and feelings people get don't just come from nowhere. On some level, people can sense things that don't belong here. Sometimes it's nothing that can be seen or harm them, but other times it's a lot more. Knowing what those things feel like will make you more aware of them. When you feel them, pay attention. If you're not sure you are, listen anyway."

"So I'm just waiting for the vibes to be off?"

He nodded cautiously. "I wouldn't put it like that, but I guess so."

"I'm never leaving my house again," she said, putting her head in her hands. "This is so insane."

"Just be careful. Does a place make you uneasy? The driver seem a little bit off? Just get out of there. It's not going to happen often, unless you're actively looking for it."

"I would never," she said. "I didn't even want to know about it at all."

"Honestly, me either. I just kind of...lucked into it."

"And then you were just like 'Hey, let me go hunt ghosts and learn magic'?"

"Not in the least," he said. "How do you think I know it works? I didn't take it and now..." He waved his hands in the air to indicate situations like these, but stopped when he saw a hefty man who definitely did not look like a doctor walk by. Henry's gaze followed him intently until he disappeared around the corner.

"Now you follow your gut, but in the opposite way," she said, nodding in the direction the man had gone.

"That's the job, like it or not," he said, standing up. "Besides, there's a lot more to follow nowadays." He smiled and patted his stomach. "In more ways than one." He turned to go and then looked back at her. The smile was gone and his expression was soft and apologetic. "I really am sorry about all this, but you really made a difference."

She didn't agree but nodded in what she hoped passed for appreciation. Henry followed after the man he'd noticed and she went back to her phone to check on flights.

***

They'd just finished setting Mark up in his hospital room when the thick and sour-faced guy strode in and studied Mark with the aura of someone who's used to being in charge. He was familiar, but before Mark could place him, he identified himself as Chief of Detectives Lobrazzo of the Cedar Ridge Police.

"I'm pretty sure Tim didn't want to press charges," Mark said, the pain in his body taking a backseat to the sudden rush of anxiety. A regular cop wouldn't have been a big deal, but someone with a fancy title showing up felt like the worst case scenario.

"That's what he said, Mr. Watson," Lobrazzo said, moving uncomfortably close to the side of Mark's bed. "But I have to tell you, I'm really having a hard time understanding exactly what happened."

"I'm not sure I follow," Mark said, hoping he was making himself look just the right amount of confused.

"Well, my understanding is you're a mechanic and not a plumber," he said, checking a handheld notebook. "That correct?"

"Yeah, but I dabble...in the plumbing. I've...plumbed." The pain killers had begun to do their job at the worst possible time.

"Sure," Lobrazzo nodded. "Who hasn't?" He went back to the notebook. "I'll hold off on asking how someone gets stabbed in the side while falling down stairs, but I'm very curious as to why you'd decide to..." he looked up a Mark with an arched eyebrow, "'plumb' at the house built on the spot where you'd nearly been killed. Allegedly."

Pain killers be damned, that jogged his memory. This was the cop who grilled him the hardest when he'd come close to being arrested for the murders back in the day. Detective Prescott had used every ounce of his pull to get Mark off the hook, but this guy had been stewing in the corner of every conversation and watching him far too closely.

"Was it?" Mark said. "I try not to think about that stuff."

"I bet." Lobrazzos eyes narrowed to tiny little pits under his eyebrows. "Is there a reason why Christine Baker, of all people, was at the scene as well? Especially since she currently resides in New Mexico?"

"Just here for a visit," Mark smiled. "Old friends and all."

"Did she also forget what happened there?"

"I...," Mark trailed off, hoping something would come to him.

"Chief Lobrazzo," Henry said, walking into the room with a disingenuous smile. "So nice to see you again."

Lobrazzo glared at him. "Mr. Churchill. What a surprise. I guess you found a way to connect with Mr. Watson after all."

"I did, and he's been very helpful. Although I'm sorry he got hurt while showing us what he's been up to nowadays."

"Doing more research for your book?" Lobrazzo said.

"I'm thinking I might put a pin in it for now. The publishing marketplace has really changed after the pandemic."

"I'm sure it has." Lobrazzo said, turning to give Henry the full weight of his gaze. "I was surprised to find out you're a private investigator and not a writer. Trying something new?"

"Everyone has to have a hobby," Henry said, smiling wider.

"I found a fascinating article about you and your lady-partner on the *New Borderlands* site. A lot of talk about ghosts, monsters, and so on."

Henry's hands were clasped behind his back and he did an exaggerated nod of embarrassed acknowledgment. "I know, and I've been trying to get them to take it down for a while. A lot of allegations and assertions without any evidence, which I think is what's called 'fake news.'"

"I bet. I was just asking Mr. Watson here--"

Henry raised a finger to stop him. "I hate to interrupt, but it's been a hell of an evening for us, and I'm pretty sure they told Mark he needed to get some rest."

Mark nodded. "Yeah, I'm pretty beat. Can we do this later or something?"

"It'll only take a moment," Lobrazzo said, not taking his eyes off of Henry. "If you don't mind?" He gestured toward the door.

"Actually," Henry said, moving around between Lobrazzo and Mark. "It's probably best Mark gets that rest, and he'll be happy to talk to you in the morning." He turned to Mark. "Right?"

"I'd really appreciate it." Mark sank down lower in the bed, like a kid trying to stay home from school. "These drugs are just...knocking me right out."

Lobrazzo narrowed his eyes. "Like I said, it'll just take a--"

"I hate to be a stickler," Henry said, taking a step forward and forcing the larger man to move back. "But I'm fairly certain that if you want to *make* him answer more questions, you're going to have to charge him with something. Honestly, I can't think of what that would be. Clumsiness, maybe?"

The detective looked down at Henry, glaring more intently. "Okay," he said. "I'll come back tomorrow morning. Hopefully you'll be more well-rested then."

"Fingers crossed," Mark said, forcing a giant yawn.

Lobrazzo left, and Henry closed the door behind him.

"Thanks," Mark said. "So much for the cops not getting wind of this."

"It was always a possibility. When we'd talked before the Chief made it clear he wasn't satisfied with how things ended before."

"Wonderful. There's no way this bullshit is going to fly if he's already suspicious. I'm fucked."

"Not necessarily," Henry said. "I'll talk to him and smooth things over."

"I'm sure that'll go over well."

"Remember," Henry winked. "I can be very persuasive. Just worry about getting better and I'll handle him."

"I can definitely multitask my worrying," Mark said. There was a soft knock at the door and Christine poked her head in. "Everything okay? That guy seemed pissed."

"It's fine," Henry said. "I just wanted to check in and say that if anything like this comes up and you need help, please don't hesitate to text me." He smiled at Christine. "I'll even fly to New Mexico. Promise."

Chapter Twelve

When Chief Detective Lobrazzo pulled into his driveway a few hours later, Henry was waiting for him.

"What the hell are you doing here?" Lobrazzo said. As soon as he saw Henry, he'd stopped in the middle of the driveway and got out, walking toward the tree Henry was leaning on.

"Hoping none of your neighbors are going to call the cops on a Black guy 'lurking in the shadows.'"

"There's an easy way to avoid that," Lobrazzo said, utilizing his "standing too close to you" tactic. Given his size Henry was sure it usually worked for him, but knowing the intent significantly lessened its effectiveness.

"Very true," Henry said. "But I wanted to talk to you about Mark Watson before you got anything in motion."

"Now you want to talk? You have some information I should know about?"

Henry shrugged. "In a sense. Just know the responsible party for those murders has been dealt with, and Mark Watson isn't involved and should be left alone."

Lobrazzo chuckled and feigned giving it some thought. "Sure, sure. You want anything else? A pony, maybe? Rocket ship?"

"I assure you I'm being serious."

"Look," Lobrazzo said, stepping even closer. "I'm sure you're very clever, but I'm telling you to let me know whatever you have or I'll charge you as an accessory after the fact."

Henry sighed. "If anything it'd be obstruction of justice. I'm really disappointed in your lack of legal knowledge, especially for a man of your station."

"You may think I can't touch you in New York, but I've got friends there. I know people who can make things *very* difficult. Given your reputation, I don't think it'd be hard." He jabbed a finger in Henry's face. "Tell me what you know."

"Here we go," Henry muttered. Before Lobrazzo could question, Henry raised his hand in front of the man's face and said "Watch this." The coin caught the light from the headlights and twinkled, catching his attention perfectly. Henry concentrated, giving just the slightest push into Lobrazzo's distracted mind. Lobrazzos's head cocked to the side and his right eye blinked rapidly, and then he slumped backward, giving Henry some space.

"You ar--"

Lobrazzo stood up straight and held up a hand to block the light reflecting into his eye.

"Knock it off," he snapped, moving up on Henry again. "Talk to me, or you're in deep shit."

Henry flipped the coin into his palm and dropped it back in his pocket. This wasn't something pushing Henry out, just an annoyingly strong will shaking off his usual light touch. That, or he'd been relying on it too much and had let himself get sloppy.

Either way, it meant he was going to have to do this the hard way.

"Okay Chief, let's calm down." Henry raised his hands, trying to make some space between them. Lobrazzo stepped forward and pushed Henry back into the tree with a meaty finger.

"You don't come to my house, threaten me, and *then* tell me to calm down. Let's see if you'll give me what I want after you've spent a night in jail." Lobrazzo reached behind his back, but then must've realized he wasn't wearing handcuffs.

"Get in the car," he said, grabbing Henry's arm.

"Stop," Henry snarled. There wasn't any build up this time, and waves of magical energy coursed through his voice.

Lobrazzo's arm fell limp at his side, and then he dropped to his knees. He made a little whimper, and then his face began to get red as he ceased breathing.

More rookie mistakes.

"Stop what he's doing, not his body."

Lobrazzo gasped for air. He reached up at Henry but his arms only moved an inch before they were held in place. The confusion on his face turned to fury.

"No talking." Lobrazzo's mouth snapped shut.

"You're going to leave Mark Watson alone. Just let it go, okay? This whole thing is over. You're going to tuck this back into the closed cases and forget all about it. I'm sure your lovely town has more important things for you to be doing."

Lobrazzo glared, terrified but defiant.

"You're not the only one with friends," Henry said, putting his face a couple of inches from Lobrazzo's. This close anyone could feel the energy coming off of him. "And mine can reach out and touch you wherever you are, understand?"

The Chief winced in pain for a moment and then the defiance was gone.

"We have a deal? Nod for yes."

Lobrazzo nodded.

Henry thought about it and then said "What does he really think?"

He winced and then roughly shook his head.

"Goddammit," Henry snapped. "Do you think I'm playing with you?"

Lobrazzo stared, wide eyed.

"You're already figuring out how to get back at me, aren't you? This just makes you more interested in the whole thing, right?" He peered over his glasses and deeper into the man's eyes. He pondered him for a few moments and then straightened up, running a hand across his scalp.

"There's just no convincing you Mark is innocent, is there? You might let it go for a bit, but one day down the road you're going to remember this and start poking around at both him and me, despite all this." Laid bare like this, Henry could feel Lobrazzo's will blocking him.

"You did this to yourself," Henry said. "Open up his mind."

Henry placed two fingers on Lobrazzo's forehead and the man's body went rigid again, this time eyes rolling back in his head. Henry plunged into the mental depths, which were immediately unpleasant. There were lies and abuse and cheating and anger, and Henry knew how easy it'd be to crush them all in his fists. He could rip and shred and make the man a halfway decent person, although not a very functional one. What was left of him would probably still be able to walk and talk, but at least he'd have empathy.

Henry refocused and looked for Mark and the Briarcliff murders. Once found, he made sure his pushing and rearranging was enough for Lobrazzo to consider everything resolved and nothing he had to think about again. He lingered, even though he knew Lobrazzo was in agony, but he told himself it was just because he was making sure he didn't miss anything.

With the mental I's dotted and T's crossed, Henry broke the connection. Lobrazzo's head slumped forward, face red and covered in sweat.

"Stand up."

Lobrazzo obliged, although quite poorly.

"Calm down. Move past the pain."

His breathing, which had been rapid and shallow, returned to normal.

"He won't remember this. He stayed in his car listening to something about sports on the radio." A simple command not requiring the strip-mining he'd just finished.

There was a small nod.

"He--," Henry caught himself before he said *--will feel that pain for the first ninety seconds after he wakes up for the rest of his life.* He pushed it back, pissed off at yet another sloppy mistake.

"Go sit in the car."

Henry followed him, and when Lobrazzo got in his car Henry said, "Released in three and a half minutes after you lose sight of me."

Lobrazzo closed the door, and Henry walked around the corner where the Gremlin was parked. Once inside, he texted Monica he was on his way, and then he navigated back to the garage.

"Watch it," he said to himself in the rear view mirror. "Don't forget who's in charge here."

Chapter Thirteen

When Henry left, Mark and Christine just stared at each other.

"At least we didn't die," Mark said, shrugging as much as he could.

She smiled a little. "I could've lived without all the trying."

"Couldn't we all." He yawned, the drugs pulling him down into sleep. "But also I think I'm going to crash. I'm sorry. For everything, not just the crashing."

"I get it," she said, walking over and taking a seat in the chair. "I'm feeling that too."

"Right on." He closed his eyes before he could invite her to "hop on in," which was probably for the best.

When he woke, he could feel how late it was. The noise of running water from the bathroom stopped and Christine came out. She'd changed clothes and put her hair up, and when she saw he was awake there was a flash of disappointment on her face.

"Hey, you're up," she said after fixing her face.

"You taking off already?"

"Yeah," she said, looking at her bag by the door. "A seat opened up on the early morning flight, and I didn't want to wake you."

"Ah," Mark said, a pit growing inside him. "I...shit, I was hoping we'd have a chance to decompress and talk about stuff."

"I get it." She took a seat on the edge of the bed. "But I really don't want to. Ever. I'm putting it behind me."

"Okay, that's fair." He gave a weak smile. "But we could still talk for a bit. Maybe you could do that remote job of yours from here for a while and nurse me back to health. It'd be fun." Hearing it out loud made him want to die a little.

"Mark," she said, putting a hand on his leg. "Coming here was a huge mistake. Yeah, we fixed shit and had some fun, but this is not a thing. And I'm not going to try to build a relationship with a guy I've known for a combined total of what, two months? Ninety percent of which was decade ago."

Mark never felt smaller. "Okay. Yeah. Message received." He could feel himself turning sour and mean, but he closed his eyes, took a breath, and pushed it away.

"It's not that I don't like you, I just--"

"No, it's silly. I shouldnt've said anything. I just...I've always wanted to see you again. When this happened, I hoped I would and it'd go...well, and I just didn't want that part to end."

She sighed and then stood up. "I think you built me up as some kind of perfect girl, and that's just not who I am. This happened because of the horrible things we went through, and now that it's out of your system or whatever you need to find a way to move on. And also get your shit together, because you're kind of a mess."

Sour and mean was starting to sound better, and it must have showed on his face.

"I know, so should I," she continued. "I've been trying my entire life, and maybe now I can actually do that." She leaned down and gave him a kiss on the top of his head. "I was wrong," she said. "You *are* a nice guy, you were just dealt a really shitty hand. Think of this a chance to start over, because that's what I'm going to do."

"Sure," he said, and true to form he could feel tears coming on. If she noticed, she didn't say anything.

She walked over to her bag, picked it up, and then turned back to say, "Take care of yourself, okay?"

"You too." He waved back, dropping it when the door closed behind her. It sucked, but she was right. There'd always been a part of him desperate to see her again and give it another shot. He'd known it was childish, but it'd been lurking under the surface for a decade. Now dredged up and laid bare before him, it was clear he'd wasted a lot of time focusing on it.

Starting over wasn't something new to him, but he realized now he could at least do it better without the what if's hanging over his head.

"Okay," he said. "Let's give it another go."

***

It took Henry a few months to relax.

He was pretty confident he kept from Monica how much things had gone wrong, so that was a relief. It wasn't like he hadn't made mistakes before, but these seemed to have piled up on each other like an accident on the highway. Next time he had to make sure he was better prepared and, most importantly, in better control.

The first feeling of relaxation dawned on him late at night as he sat in his chair in the living room, headphones on, eyes closed, and listening to his music. The summer was coming to an end, and meaning children back in school and the hope things were finally getting back to normal.

Are they though?

Henry opened his eyes. He wasn't in his living room anymore.

"I'm still mad at you," he said, glancing around at the void. "I told you, no games."

I play no games. I was just...what is it? Lending you a hand.

"You're bound to my will. Don't forget it."

There was an animalistic growl from behind him. Henry turned and saw the wall was still where it'd been for the past twenty-odd years, stretching in every direction. Not as he'd built it then, as the section across from him wasn't solid but had thick bars like a cage at the zoo.

The thing on the other side made what passed for an expression of disdain. *Don't patronize me, jailer. This was the bargain, these were the rules.*

"And the rules say I'm in control."

They do. There was a clacking along the bars as it paced in front of him. *For now. And despite how much you loathe me, you have enjoyed making use of me again. It's...exhilarating.*

"It was necessary," Henry said. "I only let you out when you're needed. And I can lock you up again if I have to."

But why would you? You wouldn't have been able to crush that insect without me, and your mind still reeks of panic when you think about why you loosed me in the first place.

"It was what I had to do. Not the best way, but the only way."

But I AM the best way. The fastest, the easiest way. Which is why you sought me out in the first place, so that I could fix what you were unable to.

"Those days are over," he said. "I've got more ways to solve problems now."

Like enchanting that girl? Is sending one of your new little charms through the phone device to push her to comply one of those new ways?

Henry gritted his teeth. "It was what I needed to do. It was the only way."

Of course, of course. Its form rippled as it made a low chuckle. *Which is why I made sure it had enough power to last. I knew how.. .important it was to you.*

"Don't you *ever* do that again," he snapped, slapping the bars between them.

It shrunk back in disingenuous fear. *Whatever you desire. I exist to serve.*

"And don't forget it," Henry said, turning and walking away. Henry was relieved he hadn't botched the charm he'd sent Christine, especially since it was an untested and recent addition to his repertoire. However, the fact that his prisoner could affect the intensity of his magic without Henry realizing did a great job of stifling said relief.

Don't you forget, jailer. I'm here because of you, and I know what you desire. You wanted to force open the mind of that insect's pawn to find out what you needed to know, and would've if you could. And you were oh so happy to torment an enforcer of laws again. I know how it's your favorite.

Henry woke up. The playlist was over and it was hours later, and he had to concentrate on releasing his grip from the arms of the chair. When his heart stopped pounding he closed his eyes, shaping what had been bars into a solid wall again. He'd been so stupid, and he'd forgotten how devious it was. It twisted desires, feigned servitude, and had always claimed to be on his side. The only side it was on was its own, and the only thing it truly desired was freedom.

And probably a lot of revenge.

Henry stood and stretched before walking back to the bedroom. He was halfway down the hall when he remembered what it was like to have the demon from Briarcliff and its minions clawing and tearing at him. When he'd fallen to his knee there was a moment when he thought it was all over, but his prisoner was able to save him. Not because it cared, but because Henry was its foothold here. As long as he lived, it got to play and torment and hurt as much as Henry would allow.

Would he be able to forgive himself if he didn't use every option available and the worst happened? Especially since he was the one who'd brought all of this into their lives. It wasn't a matter of if something that dangerous could happen, but when.

He thought about the wall, but before he did anything his phone buzzed several times in his hand. They were texts from Lexie, and reading them answered why she was sending them uncharacteristically late at night.

What's best/easiest way to kill werewolves?

Like, a whole lot of them.

Kind of an emergency.

"Goddammit," he huffed. "Why does it have to werewolves?"

Afterward

So first of all, are we feeling better about Mark's ending now? Maybe? To be fair, he's still in his twenties so things being messed up is the status quo. Your mileage may vary.

I've occasionally been asked at shows if the series has anything to do with the actual Sir Winston Churchill, as if this were some sort of Abraham Lincoln: Vampire Hunter. While maybe not a terrible idea, I'm not sure how many monsters he'd kill from his bathtub. I've also been asked if I have a special fondness for the guy, and the answer is "not really at all." I don't know where the idea of using his name for an as-of-yet unimagined pairing of characters came from, but it was just something that stuck with me. Always a slut for a thematic link, it did make naming the stories and this book easy to title. Yes, they're all fragments/slight twists on quotations of his. Yes, I was particularly chuffed at finding one that matched with "Shadow of the Past." Like my characters, I either come to books with a name in mind or I agonize over it forever.

But back to Sir Winston. Yes, very famous. Yes, helped defeat the Nazis. But also not that great a guy when it came to those under the control of the British Empire at that time, specifically in India. It is, as we saw, where the sword cane itself originated (and maybe I'll tell that story somewhere someday), so it feels appropriate to point that out. His quotes about the Bengal Famine at that time are, at best, insensitive to the millions who died during it. So that's a thing to bear in mind.

Anyway, without making too much of it, this was the fastest book I've ever written. Remember how it took twenty years for Shadow of the Past? This was about seven-eight months, tops. It's not as long as Shadow of the Past, but for me writing a short novel in that amount of time was unheard of, even just a year ago. All I can say is that when you take the time to recover from burnout, tend to your mental health, and get the right cocktail of medications, the sky's the limit. Again, it's not a brag and yes, I realized I've opened the door for people "Yeah, and it reads like you wrote it that fast too."

Part of that "time off" involved reassessing how I actually write and what was getting in my way before. I'm pretty sure I've got it figured out now, and that's really had a dramatically energizing effect on me. I'm still not smart enough to stick a single genre, format, or project at a time, but I think I'm handling it better now. I've got a lot of stuff rattlin' around in my noggin, so if it's all going to get out (and invariably make room for the new stuff that's always showing up) then I have to put in a lot of work.

Speaking of doing things the right way, my newfound focus is also helping me with that bane of every indie author, self-promotion. Despite being on the convention circuit for about six years or so, I haven't done the best of jobs building up and fostering a "fanbase." I kinda hate that word, as it's a little grandiose, so maybe "readership" is a better term. I should've been doing a lot of things differently in those days, but those just lessons I'll take to the next show I do. All that aside, it's never too late to start. I've been trying to "network" (I have that word too) with other people in the Indie Horror community, mostly with the Facebook group "Books of Horror," which was actually brought to my attention by a customer at a convention, so thanks dude.

I know Facebook is trash, but the groups are still a good way to talk to like-minded folks (don't get me started on what I think about the current state of social media as someone who was an extremely early adopter of the internet and its social aspects). I've been explore Reddit and using Discord (most specifically Cullen Bunn's very cool server) a lot more and those type platforms seem to be a lot more genuine than shooting out tweets in an algorithm that's outright hostile to anyone looking to promote themselves. Thanks to these newfound connections, I was able to do start a Beta-Reader/ARC squadron (that's what I'm calling it) of enthusiastic folks to give me a hand, both craft and social media-wise.

So my sincerest thanks to those brave souls, who include Andrew Keahey, Devin Whitlock, Stephanie Topp, Crystal Deboard, Janelle Halstead, and Amanda Jean Ruzsa to name a few.

As always, this would not have been possible without my beloved partner, Bri, Hero and Hoagie (@thesandwhichhounds), and least of all Jeffrey. You know what you did.

I hope you folks enjoyed this latest Winston & Churchill installment. The next one will be a little far off for now, so in the meantime keep up with all my goings on and possibly sign up for my mailing list and/or my Patreon maybe? All that and more, can be yours through the magic portal on the next page.

Thacher E. Cleveland,
July 2024,
Chicago, Illinois

The end of

"The Shadow of Victory"

but Lexie Winston & Henry Churchill
will return in

"A Disease of the Will"

About the Author

Thacher E. Cleveland grew up in New Jersey and upstate New York and has lived in Ohio, Tennessee, and currently resides in Chicago with his girlfriend, a criminally stupid cat, a timid rescue greyhound, and a rambunctious whippet. He writes things like novels (SHADOW OF THE PAST), short stories (The Winston and Churchill urban fantasy series) and comics (MYTHPOCALYPSE, GRIM REEFER) in various flavors of horror, science fiction, and fantasy. He's also a comic book letterer, graphic designer, and actor. He is very tired. You can find him at www.demonweasel. com, or on Instagram, Patreon, and BlueSky @demonweasel, as well as occasionally on TikTok @demonweaselstudios, even though he's too old to fit in there.

9 798991 096119